Advance Praise for
Shit Cassandra Saw

"[An] explosive, original, fearless, funny, on-the-money feminist story collection that delivers."
—*Publishers Weekly*

"When I reached the end of every single one of Gwen E. Kirby's wildly unique stories, I felt like she had altered the universe a little, created a new element, opened up some fault lines in the earth. Kirby writes with boundless humor, a confidence and ease with strange premises, and yet there is always that flash of a fang or a blade or a Sharpie, reminding you to pay closer attention."
—Kevin Wilson, *New York Times* bestselling author of *Nothing to See Here*

"*Shit Cassandra Saw* is a readable and unflinching book about womanhood in the modern world. The stories in this collection are fierce yet playful, like the characters themselves, and I read along in a fugue state of gleeful panic. Gwen E. Kirby takes readers into a fun house of the mundane, revealing the excitement, possibility, and pure fun that lives just behind the predictable man's world we already know."
—Liv Stratman, author of *Cheat Day*

"Radiant truths are arrived at raucously in *Shit Cassandra Saw*, Gwen E. Kirby's spirited debut story collection. Kirby writes with deadpan humor about louts and witches and cross-dressing pirates, gods and ghosts and whores in wildly entertaining stories that swerve into wisdom and deeply satisfy."

—Christine Schutt, author of *Pure Hollywood*

"The stories in *Shit Cassandra Saw* strike fast and leave you humming in their mysteries. Gwen E. Kirby has written a book that boldly defies categorization, much like the women at its center. Here is a writer who is too good to tell a story just one way. I'll follow Kirby's mind anywhere."

—Simon Han, author of *Nights When Nothing Happened*

PENGUIN BOOKS

SHIT CASSANDRA SAW

Gwen E. Kirby is a native San Diegan and graduate of Carleton College. She has an MFA from Johns Hopkins University and a PhD from the University of Cincinnati. Her stories appear in *One Story, Tin House, Guernica, Mississippi Review, Ninth Letter, SmokeLong Quarterly,* and elsewhere. Currently, she is the Associate Director of Programs and Finance for the Sewanee Writers' Conference at the University of the South, where she also teaches creative writing.

SHIT
CASSANDRA
SAW

GWEN E. KIRBY

STORIES

PENGUIN BOOKS

PENGUIN BOOKS

An imprint of Penguin Random House LLC

penguinrandomhouse.com

Copyright © 2022 by Gwen E. Kirby

"Shit Cassandra Saw That She Didn't Tell the Trojans Because at
That Point Fuck Them Anyway," *SmokeLong Quarterly*, issue 55,
March 2017. Also appears in *Best Small Fictions* 2018.

"A Few Normal Things That Happen a Lot," *Tin House* online,
October 31, 2018, part of Tin House of Horrors.

"Jerry's Crab Shack: One Star," *Mississippi Review*, vol. 44/1&2, summer 2016.

"Mt. Adams at Mar Vista," *One Story*, issue 240, April 19, 2018.

"Friday Night," *Wigleaf*, April 6, 2019.

"First Woman Hanged for Witchcraft in Wales, 1594,"
New Delta Review, issue 7.2, spring 2017.

"Casper," *Alaska Quarterly Review*, summer/fall 2020, vol. 37, no. 1 & 2.

"An Apology of Sorts to June," *MonkeyBicycle*, May 12, 2017.

"The Disneyland of Mexico," *Southwest Review*, vol. 100, issue 1, 2015.

"For a Good Time, Call," *Hobart*, December 15, 2016.

"Inishmore," *Ninth Letter*, vol. 12, no. 2, fall/winter 2015–2016.

"The Best and Only Whore of Cwm Hyfryd, Patagonia,
1886," *Blackbird*, spring 2019, vol. 18, no. 1.

"Midwestern Girl Is Tired of Appearing in Your Short
Stories," *Guernica*, October 18, 2017.

"Scene in a Public Park at Dawn, 1892," *Fractured Lit*, forthcoming.

"How to Retile Your Bathroom in 6 Easy Steps!"
Cincinnati Review, fall 2019, vol. 16, no. 2.

"We Handle It," *New Ohio Review*, issue 20, fall 2016.

LIBRARY OF CONGRESS CATALOGING-IN-PUBLICATION DATA
Names: Kirby, Gwen E., author.
Title: Shit Cassandra saw : stories / Gwen E. Kirby.
Description: New York : Penguin Books, 2022.
Identifiers: LCCN 2021018004 (print) | LCCN 2021018005 (ebook) |
ISBN 9780143136620 (trade paperback) | ISBN 9780525508120 (ebook)
Subjects: LCGFT: Short stories.
Classification: LCC PS3611.I724 S48 2022 (print) |
LCC PS3611.I724 (ebook) | DDC 813/.6—dc23
LC record available at https://lccn.loc.gov/2021018004
LC ebook record available at https://lccn.loc.gov/2021018005

Printed in the United States of America
1st Printing

Set in Sabon LT Pro

Designed by Alexis Farabaugh

for my sister Claire

you more than anyone

you more than anything

"You speak like a heroine," said Montoni, contemptuously; "we shall see whether you can suffer like one."

—ANN RADCLIFFE, *THE MYSTERIES OF UDOLPHO*

CONTENTS

SHIT CASSANDRA SAW

SHIT CASSANDRA SAW THAT SHE DIDN'T TELL THE TROJANS BECAUSE AT THAT POINT FUCK THEM ANYWAY

Lightbulbs.

Penguins.

Bud Light.

Velcro.

Claymation. The moon made out of cheese.

Tap dancing.

Yoga.

Twizzlers. Mountain Dew. Jell-O. Colors she can eat with her eyes.

Methamphetamine.

T-shirts. Thin and soft, they pass from person to person, men to women, each owner slipping into different teams—Yankees, Warriors—and out again with no bloodshed, no thought to allegiance or tribe. And the words! Profusions of nonsense. The Weather Is Here, Wish You Were Fine. Chemists Do It on the Table Periodically. Cut Class Not Frogs. Words everywhere and for everyone, for nothing but a joke, for the pleasure of them, a world so careless with its words. And not just on T-shirts. Posters. Water bottles. Newspapers. Junk mail. Bumper stickers. Lists. Top ten Halloween costumes for your dog as modeled by this corgi. Top ten times a monkey's facial expression perfectly summed up your thoughts on NAFTA. Top ten things your boyfriend *wishes* you would do in bed but is too afraid to say. Cassandra has not noticed a lack of men telling women what to do. Perhaps this will be a pleasure of the future, a male desire that goes *un*spoken. A desire that is only a desire, and not a command.

Then there are the small words, the private words, hidden within romance novels, mysteries, thrillers, science fiction, fantasy. Heaving bosoms, astronauts, and ape men. Pulp paperbacks that live brief but fiery lives, the next torrent of words so swift behind they must sell or be destroyed, only enough space on the shelf for the new.

And lives, of course. Cassandra would rather see only the fictions, the objects, the colored plastic oddities of the future, but she must see lives as well. Here are two little girls. They sit in the dirt and dig at a boulder. When it is finally unearthed, the possibilities! A passage to the underworld, a buried treasure, a colony of fairies—anything but dirt. It is essential that they will never succeed, never dig up the boulder, and of course they don't. Their plastic shovels move the dirt aside; new dirt, dusty and thin, blows across their eyes. One of the girls becomes an engineer. One is raped by her college boyfriend. This second girl will run a bakery on an island where she loves to hike. She will have three children, all boys, and she will die when she is quite old and quite unwilling to go. Her boys will have lives too. Everyone does. Lives on fast forward, on silent, even the best life, even her own, swiftly boring.

Cassandra is tired of running at wooden horses with nothing but the flame of the smallest match.

She is tired of speaking to listening ears. The listening ears of the men who think her mad drive her to madness. She wishes she could move far away to an island and own a bird. She will never do this because she knows she never does. It is said that Apollo gave Cassandra the gift of prophecy—this is true. It is said that, when she refused his advances, he spit in her mouth so that she would never again be believed. A virgin the same as a seduced woman the same as a violated woman the same as a willing woman, all women opening their mouths to watch snakes slither out and away.

Cassandra is *done*, full the fuck up, soul weary.

Still, as Troy is sacked, as she clings to the cold marble legs of the statue of Athena in the sacred temple, she cannot accept what she knows to be true. That soon, Ajax will arrive and rape her. He will smash the statue of the goddess she worships and curse his own life; and worse, her goddess will not help her, will turn her shattered face away. Cassandra will be carried across the sea, made another man's concubine, bear twin boys, and be killed by Clytemnestra. But before this comes to pass, there are visions Cassandra burns to share with the women of Troy.

The women of Troy might listen. They know that Cassandra's curse is their curse as well. That Apollo spit in her mouth, but it was only spit.

Here is what she might show them.

Tampons.

Jeans.

Washing machines.

The cordless Hitachi Magic Wand.

Elastic hair ties.

Mace.

Epidurals.

And here is the best thing of all, the thing that makes Cassandra smile as the men storm her temple, exactly as she has always known they would: someday, Trojan

will not be synonymous with bravery or failure, be-
trayal or endurance, or the most beautiful woman or
the most foolish of men. A Trojan will be carried in
every hopeful wallet, extracted with abashed confidence, slipped over the shaft, rolled to the base. Perhaps
the Trojan men would laugh if they knew, or be humili-
ated, or pause to think about the indifference of history
and the hubris of the man who hopes to be remembered.
But the women, once they saw that blue streamer un-
furl, the women would rejoice, would wave it over their
heads like a new flag, like a promise of better things to
come.

A FEW NORMAL THINGS
THAT HAPPEN A LOT

A woman walks down the street and a man tells her to smile. When she smiles, she reveals a mouthful of fangs. She bites off the man's hand, cracks the bones and spits them out, and accidentally swallows his wedding ring, which gives her indigestion.

A woman waits for the bus and a man stands too close to her. He puts his hand on her ass, with no idea that she is the first successful subject of a top-secret science experiment. She turns and points her laser eyes at him and transforms him into bus fare: two dollars and seventy-five cents in cool coins.

A woman is at the grocery store and a man in the frozen food aisle says, "Nice legs." He follows her past the broccoli and peas. "What's a pretty girl like you doing here alone?" Past the tubs of Cool Whip. "You got a boyfriend?" Past the ice-cream cakes. "Don't you want to say something nice?" She stops at the endcap. There's a sale on chips and salsa. Yesterday, she would not have acknowledged him. She would have moved on, feigned fascination with the cheeses, lingered over the pasta sauce, waited for the man to get bored. She would have left, buying nothing, the dark parking lot endless, every car disguising a threat.

Luckily, last night she was bitten by a radioactive cockroach. Underneath her clothes, she is covered in armor. He asks, "You shy or just a bitch?" Her senses are heightened. She hisses at a decibel that shatters the jars of salsa, studding the man's chest with small shards of glass. Salsa splatters everywhere and a chunk of tomato lands on the hem of her skirt, which is sad, because she just had it dry-cleaned. In the dark, arms full of groceries, the parking lot is beautiful in a way she's never noticed before. A fine rain drifts across the weak lights. The asphalt shimmers, and the cars hide *nothing*.

A woman sits alone in her apartment where she can hear her neighbor, who is drunk, banging down the hall. She does not check her lock, tug the chain to make sure it's secure. Instead, she picks up her remote control, given to her by a witch. If anyone tries to come inside, she will point the remote control at the door and turn him off.

A woman jogs on a cold day and a man jogs fifty, thirty, twenty feet behind her. They are the only two people on this path, a narrow ribbon tracing the river. It's her favorite place to run. She speeds up, and so does he. Her heart begins to hammer and she curses herself, *stupid bitch, people have told you not to run alone, you know better, stupid bitch*, but then she remembers, *thank god!* Very recently, she was scratched by a werewolf! The woman allows herself to change a little bit, turns to the man, and pulls off her gloves. Her hands are covered in fur, the paw pads black and leathery, and when she extends her claws the man yelps and runs away. The woman rubs her cold cheeks with her soft fur. She breathes deeply and falls back into an even pace.

———

A woman is on the subway and a man sits right next to her even though there are many empty seats. The woman folds her small hands in her lap. The man takes out his dick and begins to masturbate. The woman stands and exits at the next stop. The woman's heart is *not* racing, she does not feel nauseous, and she does not wonder what she would have done if the man had followed her.

No, once she steps onto the platform and the subway doors close behind her, the woman never thinks about the man ever again. This is her superpower, bestowed upon her as a baby by her alien mother. She feels absolutely fine, and she even does bit of work in the early evening before deciding she's tired and ordering Chinese. She sleeps deeply.

A woman goes on a date with a man and while they are walking to the restaurant, they see another woman bite off another man's hand. The man on the date rushes to the man on the ground, who is bleeding profusely. The woman on the date asks where the biting woman got those fangs. "They look great on you," she says.

"Do you think so?" the other woman asks. "They're

exactly what I needed for that extra boost of confidence."

For the rest of the date, the man with two hands is extremely respectful.

The cockroach woman goes to the bank and hopes someone will rob it, so she has an excuse to use her new and amazing powers. Instead, the man in front of her is having a conversation with a woman and he interrupts her. "The thing is," the man says, "it's just too easy to *generalize*, you know?" The cockroach woman considers ripping off the man's arm, but that would be an overreaction. She deposits a check and feels glum as she walks to work, her newly grown antennae vibrating in the breeze.

The same man from before takes his dick out on the subway. He is sitting next to the woman with a mouthful of fangs. She freezes for a moment in disbelief, but it's really happening, it's really happening, and so she leans over and bites off his dick. She spits it out. No bones in it to break. She leaves it, harmless, on the floor and gets off at the next stop. She keeps her face calm— she is accustomed to ignoring the screams and the blood—but the taste lingers in her mouth all the way home.

The woman with the magical remote control carries it with her everywhere, in her purse next to her pepper spray and a half eaten bag of M&Ms tightly twisted closed. She would never use the remote in public; there is no way to be sure that she'd hit her target. In a recurring nightmare, a man is yelling at her for messing up his order, a two-shot half-caf *skim* latte you stupid cunt and in her anger she shuts off the entire coffee shop, the entire block, the whole world, and she presses rewind, *rewind*, but it's too late.

As she walks down the street, she enjoys a fantasy in which she slips her hand into her purse and presses pause. In the still city, she can do anything she wants. She walks for miles, down small alleys, through wooded parks, past the corner where the homeless man yells obscenities, but see, he's quiet now. She's brought them both peace.

Werewolf-woman has never before loved being in her body, but now she shakes her fur out whenever she is home. She's at her most powerful when she's naked.

Sometimes, late at night, she stands in the backyard and howls—not because she is sad, but because her lungs are strong and it is a joy to turn air into sound. Her husband sees how happy she is and he asks her to scratch him, to turn him too. She *wants* to want to. She tries to explain to him that this is kind of *her* thing, that she needs this thing for herself. What she can't find the courage to say is that she needs it to *not* be for him. He says he understands, but she knows he'll never quite forgive her.

The fanged woman eats a donut on a park bench, although the fangs make it difficult. She is in a bad mood. Her tongue is sore, her cheeks nipped raw, and her blazer is dusted in powdered sugar. She wishes a man would make some comment so she could bite him, but nobody does. The fangs, after all, are easy to see.

She calls her friend, the woman who forgets. "Most days I'm fine," she says, her *s*'s emerging with a slight sibilance. "It's just days like today, I'm tired."

"That sounds terrible," her friend says, though she wishes they weren't always talking about men. The friend who forgets picks at a seed stuck in her dull teeth. The woman with fangs dusts crumbs off her fingers and says she needs to go.

———

A woman walks down the hallway of a large academic building after hours. She is eighteen, a freshman, and at least once a week since she's been at school she has received a mass email from the college about a sexual assault in the area. At the bottom of every email is a bulleted list of ways to keep herself from harm. Despite the warnings not to be alone at night, she is there to pick up a paper from her professor's mailbox. When she gets to the mailroom, the door is locked. All this for nothing, and here is the stairwell again. When she was fourteen, a man in a stairwell stopped her to ask a question, pressed her against a wall, groped her breasts. She runs down the stairs, empty tonight except for the men she peoples them with, and they reach for her like the branches in Snow White's dark forest. She hates that she is such a coward, and is angry for calling herself a coward.

If her imagination were not occupied, she would notice a twenty-dollar bill on the final landing. She would pick up the money and spend it on a novel or a movie, maybe pay back a friend for lunch. Later that night, a sophomore man finds the money as he is walking calmly down the stairs. He thinks about a movie he's going to make with his friends, which they will shoot in the park at night while getting high. He will enter it in the college film festival and place second. Years later, he is a director of indie films.

Luckily for the woman, she arrives home safely and the next day she is bitten by a radioactive cockroach. Radioactive cockroaches are sweeping the city. She loves her new powers, but she doesn't know how to tell the man she is dating about all the changes to her body. They break up.

The woman who watched the woman with fangs bite off a man's hand gets fangs for herself. She snaps them at her reflection in the mirror. There is blood on the fangs just like she imagined, except it's her own blood, from where her gums are still aching and raw.

The government finds out about the radioactive cockroaches after the mayor's wife is bitten in her sleep. The mayor, though he shares a bed with his wife, is unbitten and unchanged. What a strange thing! What is happening? No one knows! And the infection is spreading quickly. The mayor's wife is taken in for testing. The press reports that she has fallen ill and is taking some time out of the public eye. On Reddit, conspiracy theories grow and tangle like vines.

———

A woman walks down the street and absolutely no one bothers her. She smiles at the other women she passes. They smile back. Something is different.

A woman wears a pair of fake antennae to take out the trash to the alley behind her building, where she's always been too afraid to go at night. No one bothers her, except for a large rat, who is plump and resentful.

Now that she can pretend to be a cockroach, the woman with fangs considers having the teeth removed but, in the end, she has grown too used to feeling safe. What if the radioactive cockroaches prove *not* to be the answer? What if someone invents a special cockroach taser? What if the scientists who are hard at work discover a cure? She keeps her fangs and accepts that her mouth will always be a little sore.

Fake antennae sales skyrocket. The men of the city do not feel safe. The women of the city play. They draw baths and hold their breath under the water for thirty minutes, testing the depths of their new lungs. They get very drunk on the beer that their cockroach bodies love, and walk home under the stars, and when they see a man they hiss and the man runs away and they laugh and laugh. "Can't you take a joke?" they shriek, and they almost feel bad, because two wrongs don't make a right. But one wrong after wrong and wrong and wrong and wrong *does* make a cockroach woman feel better, reckless, free.

Men carry small cans of Raid in their pockets when they go out at night. It isn't enough, not by a long shot, but the men hold the cans tightly in their hands, like talismans. With all women wearing antennae now, there is no way to tell which ones may actually be dangerous.

The woman who forgets and the woman with fangs get coffee and the woman who forgets tells the woman with fangs that she doesn't understand this new fashion trend.

"I tried on a pair," she says, "but they flattened my hair and gave me a headache."

The woman with fangs is on antibiotics. One of her teeth has developed an abscess.

"Headaches are the worst," she says, and begins to cry.

A man cuts off the head of his cockroach girlfriend while she's sleeping. She staggers upward, attacks and kills him, and still has a whole week left to live. She walks down the city streets holding her head under her arm so that she can see where she's going. She writes an article for *BuzzFeed* about embracing the time she has left, but the truth is, her severed throat is tight with terror. She wishes she had died three days ago, that she'd never become a cockroach to begin with. There is nothing worse than knowing that the man she loved cut off her head, except the fact that killing him has not made her whole again.

Two women inventors are in their secret lab full of radioactive cockroaches. They wear long white coats and thick goggles. Their red rubber gloves go up to their elbows.

"I hope we did the right thing," one of them says as she gently injects a new serum into a cockroach, then places him in jar #B872.

"I think buying the changing table for Marianna was

the perfect choice," the other replies, her head bent over a beaker, waiting for the orange liquid to cool.

They work long hours and are always relieved when it's time to go home. They talk about plans for the evening as they peel off their goggles and gloves and coats. Under their clothes, they are mosaics of failed experiments. Scars across cheeks, toenails hardened into claws, patches of skin turned to stone and fur and scales. One woman has the interlocking armor of an armadillo down her spine. The other has a single wing that can't unfold all the way; the feathers clog her shower drain.

The women step outside, put on their fake antennae, and walk home holding hands. A man coming toward them nods respectfully and gives them a wide berth. They smile at each other, not evil smiles, but not nice ones, either. They feel good and safe, but not as good and safe as they'd imagined they would. They are distracted from the stars and the cool night air by the places on their bodies that burn and pull and pinch, the itching that never stops. They are proud of what they've done. But still, sometimes, they wish they could be smooth and whole, some softer version of themselves.

JERRY'S CRAB SHACK: ONE STAR

Gary F.
Baltimore, MD
Yelp member since July 14, 2015

Review: Jerry's Crab Shack
Review posted: July 15, 2015, 2:08 am

After perusing this restaurant's website and reading the positive reviews on Yelp, my wife and I went to Jerry's Crab Shack this evening. We did not have a good experience. It was not "a home run," as another reviewer wrote. I don't know where these reviewers usually go to dinner, and I won't post the speculations I typed and then deleted because they were unflattering and, dare I say, so accurate as to be hurtful and it is not my intention to be hurtful. I simply want to correct the record.

I'm going to review Jerry's Crab Shack in a methodical, fair-minded manner so that other people who use this site, people like my wife and me, who are new to Baltimore and *rely* on this site to make informed dinner plans, can know what they are getting into and make their own decisions. If you are going to take the time to do something, as my dear wife says, do it right or don't bother, and let her do it like she does everything else (ha ha).

*Location

Jerry's Crab Shack is near Fell's Point (not *in* historic Fell's Point, as their website says). In fact, the "shack," which is not a shack but a regular storefront wedged between a hair salon and a mattress store, is several blocks to the east, in a less-than-savory part of the neighborhood. If after reading this, you, future Yelp user, still plan to go to Jerry's Crab Shack, I would suggest that you do not park your car near Jerry's. Park in Fell's Point proper and walk. Even if you are mugged, the criminals will only take your wallet and not, as happened to us, your front right window (shattered), your

Garmin navigation system, and five CDs, including a Smithsonian Folkways two-CD set, *Rhythms of Rapture: Sacred Musics of Haitian Vodou*, that you were looking forward to listening to on your commute.

*Décor

Jerry's seems all right when you first walk in. I said this review would be fair, and I meant it. Some people don't know how to separate their feelings about a thing from the thing itself, but I do. That is why I am willing to admit that even if *I* did not enjoy the sensation that is *Avatar* in 3-D, and even if *I* do not understand the appeal of jogging, they both have value independent of me. Just because hard-boiled eggs make everything in the refrigerator smell like hard-boiled eggs and that smell triggers my sensitive gag reflex, I understand why some people might feel differently and would want to eat them for breakfast every day. Different strokes, etc.

Jerry's commits to its nautical theme. The bar has charming fishing net draped above it, and caught in the net are plastic starfish and a cardboard mermaid. On the walls are pictures of sailboats, not framed but tacked to the plaster, the edges curled and yellowing as they might be in a more authentically briny atmosphere. At the end of the bar is a rubber crab, lovingly cuddled up to a Bud

Light. A sign next to it says: "No One Feels Crabby with a Bud Light!" (You can definitely feel crabby with a Bud Light. I would argue, considering all the better beers out there in the world, that you *should* feel crabby with a Bud Light. I would also say that since the staff of Jerry's Crab Shack seems so invested in their status as "native" Baltimoreans, they might consider supporting Maryland businesses and serving only local beers.)

There are eight tables, covered with laminated red-and-white-check tablecloths. Ours had holes in it, through which you can feel the soft white polyester fuzz. We were expecting more of a "restaurant restaurant" (my wife's words), and less of a "bar with some tables" (also my wife). The pictures on the website do *not* accurately reflect the interior, so this was not my fault. I was lead to expect more of a nautical bistro atmosphere, which my wife later insisted was "not a thing." The point is, I promised my wife a special dinner. I told her this place would be "quintessentially Baltimore." I hoped that we would finally be able to unwind and enjoy an evening out of the house, away from the half unpacked boxes and nearly empty rooms.

*Cleanliness

Not the cleanest.

While waiting to be seated (before we realized this was more of a seat-yourself establishment), I watched my wife lift her heel, up and down, again and again, testing the fly-strip stickiness of the floor. Her face got that set look I recognize. *It's so authentic*, I said, hoping to cut off any potential negativity at the pass. (I was noticing and appreciating the already-mentioned netting as well as the bathroom doors labeled Pirate and Lady Pirate, which I found very egalitarian.) Janet—my wife's name is Janet—can get it in her head to not like a thing and then there is no changing her mind. The woman could be unhappy at her own birthday party (which she has been, multiple times). So the place wasn't the cleanest! I would think that with the word shack in the title, you'd have been forewarned.

The floor could use a mop. They could stand to "swab the decks." But our table was wiped down, and we did not see any cockroaches. My wife would say that that is a low bar to set for cleanliness, so I will also add that I saw a sign saying they had passed their health inspection and that that sign was hung prominently in the window, where it is legally required to be.

*Service

Service was, at first, fine. A woman too old to be wearing a pirate wench costume welcomed us and took our order—two softshell crab sandwiches (according to Yelp, their "star" dish) and a side of slaw. Her wench bodice (though maybe I should say Lady Pirate bodice) was black faux leather and her breasts overfilled it, not the way young breasts do, pushing plumply up and over, but like balloons that have begun to lose some helium, balloons three days after the party.

(I want to pause here a moment and say that I do not normally complain about restaurant service. As the child of a father who complained, loudly and ad nauseam, about slow waitresses, unfriendly waitresses, slutty waitresses, indeed, as a boy too often embarrassed by the impatience and insensitivity of an authority figure, I usually take a bit of bad service on the chin. Waitresses are people too, and not every meal I eat has to be the best I've ever eaten. I've choked down a few dinners in my life and kept my mouth shut about it. My wife is perhaps a little less forgiving, a little prone to complain when food comes out cold or I forget to buy milk at the store even when I promised I would remember, but she really only complains when it is warranted. She does not let people "walk all over her," and I "shouldn't either." What happened tonight was not the waitress's fault. I don't know what my father expects. Waitresses are not wizards. All I expect from them is the transportation of food from one point to a different point, and they don't even need to smile because what in the hell is there to smile about when you are working as a waitress at Jerry's Crab Shack and your manager has you stuffed into a corset two sizes too small and you have three kids at home and corns on your feet and two people in their DC-black suits sit down in your section and one of them asks whether the crabs are locally sourced, which of course they are, which is why that woman looked at us like we were morons and clearly not from around here even though we are now local homeowners.)

Food took forty-five minutes. Or, rather, I should say: after forty-five minutes, things at the table had become tense. We were both tired and very hungry. Moving is a lot of work. There have been more than a few nights spent eating leftover pizza on the floor because the new table we ordered online is stuck in a warehouse in St. Louis and even when my wife called the company and used her most terrifying voice they told her that we would have to wait, that they were working on it. We had both been looking forward to this dinner.

Are they sending someone out to catch *the crabs first?* Janet said, and I knew she was about to stand up and ask where our food was. So I got up first, to avoid making a scene. I hate drama in restaurants. I hate it a lot. I may have snapped at Janet before going over to the bar, but that was kind of on her, since she knows how much I hate when people bother waitresses.

(You know, Janet has a lot of good qualities. I want to say that right now. This is not a review of my wife.)

If this were a review of my wife, I might review her based on:

1) Supportiveness

2) Empathy

3) Stability

4) Sense of humor

5) Physical appearance

6) Tolerance for me

Janet is supportive. When I wanted to go to graduate school for a masters in musicology, she said I should do it, and then she paid for it even though we weren't married yet. (Janet is a lawyer.) I think supporting her then-long term boyfriend's masters in musicology also speaks to her empathy, because when you tell people you are a musicologist they mostly look at you like you are insane or you made up your job. She did not do that. She loves that I love music and that I work for Smithsonian Folkways, which is my dream job, and so what if I now live an hour-and-a-half commute away from that dream job and can't go out with coworkers after work because she wants to own a house, which we can't afford to do in DC, and have children.

Obviously, I want those things too.

Janet is very stable. You could call her a boulder. A flat-bottomed boulder. Not that she has a flat bottom. (Rating her on attractiveness I give her a 10++.) What I mean is, you couldn't roll her down a hill or something because she isn't that type of boulder. When she says she is going to do something, she does it. If she had said we were going to a nice restaurant, we would have shown up at Jerry's to discover white linens and locally sourced cocktail bitters. Sometimes I think she simply wills things into being with the force of her mind.

She also has a wonderful sense of humor. When we walked into Jerry's Crab Shack and she saw the rubber crab, she smiled.

The only item about which I might have anything at all negative to say would be number 6) Tolerance for me, and really only tolerance for me lately. She is "all in" about our move to Baltimore. If I "had doubts," I should have "said something before we *bought* the goddamn house and moved all our shit up here." I don't disagree with that. She just doesn't see that I am both all in, in the sense that I am sure she knows what's best, and not all in, in the sense that I am not sure what will happen next or that I'll like it.

*Service (bar)

And here we get to the crux of the issue. I don't know where Jerry hires his bar staff, but they are the rudest, most unpleasant people on the face of the earth.

I walked over to the bar and asked the bartender, politely, when our food might be ready. And this bartender, someone obviously on work release from a local prison, or recently kicked out of his biker gang for being too obnoxious, tells me it'll *be ready when it's ready.* Then, he rather grudgingly looked over at the order-up window and said, *soon probably.* I realize that doesn't sound so bad. In retrospect, it seems pretty reasonable. But I could not go back to the table and tell Janet that the food would be out "soon probably." I needed a timetable. Or a reason the food was being so slow. A kitchen fire, a death in the chef's family, a sudden crab shortage sweeping the Chesapeake. I had already screwed up dinner. I was going to be assertive. This was the one thing I could do right for her. So I said, *Can you go back and check? Or find our waitress?* And he said, *I've got a bar to tend, dude. Unless you want a drink, I got other customers to worry about.* The other men at the bar were starting to look at me. I could see them judging me, for my suit and the way I hold myself, which I know is a little awkward. I have unusually long arms. I said, *This is simply unacceptable*, again, not because I felt that it was that unacceptable but because I wanted to make Janet happy. I think I asked to speak to Jerry. My voice may have gone up in volume. That was when the bartender said that *I should sit the fuck down in my faggy DC suit and wait like everyone else.* The other men sitting at the bar laughed that rumbling masculine chuckle, as if something funny had happened, and they laughed again when the bartender accused me of "blushing." I did not say anything back because there isn't anything to say to that kind of behavior. I absolutely do not regret not saying anything at that moment and simply walking back to my table.

I don't know what people in this city have against DC. Not everyone from DC is an asshole. And I'm not even from DC. I'm from Ohio.

It feels good to have gotten that off my chest. I don't want to lie to you, future Yelp reader. I feel like we are connecting, really unburdening ourselves. I'll tell you a few more things. I am drinking a beer right now, my third, and it is only just beginning to help. My wife went to sleep hours ago. I am sitting with my computer, the empty bottles, and a little lamp on the wooden floor of what will be the living room because I don't have a desk yet and I don't want to go upstairs. This isn't where I hoped I would be. I was hoping to have "an extra special" night. And by *extra* special, I mean I hoped I would be having sex. There, I said it. I don't have a problem talking about natural acts between a man and his wife. Unlike the bartender, I am not so insecure about my sexuality that I have to resort to inappropriate homophobic name-calling. It did not make me feel good to be called "faggy" in front of my wife. It made me feel shitty. I do not like that bartender's comment repeating in my head.

I actually do have a problem talking about sex sometimes. I could say that I used a euphemism for sex because I didn't want to shock more conservative Yelp users by talking about the beast with two backs, but the truth is, there are moments (like right now) when being a person in a body seems impossible. All the parts working in chorus, repetitive involuntary rhythms, a near miracle of coordination. Bodies are strange, so fleshy and pierceable. Sometimes when I am on my endless commute I think about the parts of my car which, in an accident, would be most likely to run me through. The steering column. The parking brake. A shard from the other car. I don't like to think about how thin a membrane my skin actually is, but once I get it in my head, it's hard to get it out. This is why I am upset about the loss of my CDs.

Have you ever listened to Haitian Vodou music? It's not what you would expect. A low patter of rain beat out on the drum. The song a chant, one woman leading, the village following. Call and response. They invite the spirits to come and ride them. But in the end, it's the music that rides you.

I don't know how I got here.

Janet has an outie belly button. It's cute, like a little pigtail on her stomach. She hates it. And she doesn't like when I touch it. She says it "feels weird," as if I am poking a sensitive cord that sends shocks to a place in her body she can't name, a secret nestling between her uterus and stomach. It is hard to fuck someone and not rub up against their outie belly-button. Also, because I know I can't touch it, sometimes touching it is the only thing I can think about.

Janet doesn't use sites like Yelp. She isn't like me and you. She doesn't trust random people's opinions. She reads food critics, peruses "Best of" lists. Since we moved here, she has started to read the *Baltimore Sun*. She does her research and she has high standards. I like this about her.

If Janet were reviewing me, I wonder what criteria she would use. I think she would say that I make her laugh.

I think she would say she finds me handsome instead of saying that I *am* handsome. I think she would use the word "frustrated" and bring up small things: taking out the trash, removing expired food from the refrigerator, planning dates. I hope she would say that I am loyal and that she would rank that quality above all others, because I think it's the best one I have. I think if she understood that, she'd see why I didn't raise a fuss about moving here, why I go along with her when maybe I should speak up. I worry that perhaps she likes this quality in me least of all.

*Food

We left after the incident at the bar. When I sat back down, neither of us said anything. We waited five minutes. I hoped she would make a scene, which I have never hoped for before in a restaurant, but she just twisted her napkin in silence. I said I thought we should call it a night and we picked up Wendy's on the way home and ate it in the car. So I cannot speak to the quality of the food at Jerry's Crab Shack. If it is truly the best softshell crab in the city, then we will never eat the best softshell crab in the city. We will always settle for second best, and probably not even know the difference.

BOUDICCA, MIGHTY QUEEN OF THE BRITAINS, CONTACT HITTER AND UTILITY OUTFIELDER, AD 61

I like to think that if I'd been born today and, as this is my hypothetical scenario, born a man, I would be a professional baseball player. When I step up to bat for the Milwaukee Brewers, the fans cheer *Booooooo* because it's a joke, you know, *Booooooooudicca, beloved Booooooudicca*, and unlike when the men cheer my name and we ride into battle, no one dies and I hit a double and put myself in scoring position. You thought I'd say a home run? No. When you are an oppressed army fighting invading Romans, you don't go for the big swing, don't balance your home runs with a high strike-out percentage, because a strike-out means you are dead and dead and dead and there is already enough of that.

It isn't that I want to be a man, it's just that if I were playing professional baseball, my long hair would get in my eyes and my tits would hamper my swing. Kidding! My tits never get in the way when I'm stabbing Romans. They don't get in the way when I fuck or cook or turn cartwheels under the full moon. No, I just don't want to overthink my fantasy and so I let myself be a man with a man's stride, like he's always got to waddle a bit to avoid pinching his cock. I'd walk up to bat for the Seattle Mariners and the fans would yell *Booooooo* and I'd know I could never let them down and I'd hit a single but with a man on third and he'd get in nice and easy, wouldn't even have to slide, that's the best kind of battle, when you get them before they even know to raise their weapons.

It isn't that I want to be a man, except for the obvious other advantages. For example, when my husband King Prasutagus left our kingdom to me and my daughters, the Romans looked for the elephant trunk between my legs and, missing that, seeing in its place a more complicated piece of machinery, they decided to express their insecurity by killing

---

yes, killing, but even to stop all of that I could not wish to be a man, I will not wish to be a man, no matter how many lives it saves, because it is not fair that I should change to suit the desires of others. So I go to the plate as a woman, I wear my armor when I step up to the plate for the San Diego Padres and the crowd shouts *Boooooooo* and *Booooooooodicca* and I hit a home run and shock them all, because I am a practical hitter, a contact hitter, I play for the glory of the team, I'm willing to get hit by the pitch to get on base, but today I've risked it all, swung big and hard and I run the bases screaming a battle cry until my throat is raw.

MT. ADAMS AT MAR VISTA

The Mt. Adams varsity softball team warms up in right field, throwing yellow balls back and forth in sunny arcs. They try to be quiet, but they cannot stop their chatter as their shoulders loosen. The field is a good one. The grass is close cut, the bases bright, and the brick dugouts painted red and navy, the home team's colors. It is nicer than the Mt. Adams ballpark, with its dugout full of weeds and half-eaten sunflower seeds. The girls like to see how far they can spit the uncracked shells, sucking off the salt first and then aiming them through the diamonds of the fence.

It is a perfect day for a game except that everything is wrong. All week, adults have plagued them. *How do you feel about playing Mar Vista? Do you want to talk about it? It's so soon*—and in this pause fall all the words they don't say. *Shooting, death.* Ms. Matheson, the Mt. Adams AP chemistry teacher, gets teary-eyed and looks at her students too hard, like she is trying to preserve them in amber with her stare. Mr. Grater, the eleventh-grade English teacher, tells them they will understand it more, and differently, when they are older, which they suppose must be true, but also must be true of everything. What they understand right now is that these conversations are warnings as much as anything else. How the girls *should* feel, the adults convey with every softened syllable, is sensitive to the tragedy. And they should be on their best behavior. They should feel respectful and aware and appreciative of the other team's courage. The fact that those girls are even playing, it is made clear, is a victory for them. *Everyone is a winner on this field today*, said Coach Jeff as the girls unpacked their gear in the dugout, hanging bats and knocking dirt out of their helmets. And while this is true before the game starts, it cannot be true by the time the game ends.

The Mar Vista girls warm up in left field.

How do the girls of Mt. Adams varsity softball actually feel? Molly feels sympathy but nothing stronger. This shooting was closer to her school than the one in Philadelphia or the one in Ohio, but in the end, it still wasn't at *her* school. When she tries to make herself feel upset, nothing will really come until she thinks about her grandmother dying. That is as close as Molly has been to tragedy and she is embarrassed but grateful. Lisa worries that her parents are fighting a lot lately. Simone feels too much when she looks at the picture of the dead student, a freshman who looks like her own freshman brother. She looks at the picture often. She cries well and easily and this means that when she is not looking at the picture, she feels fine. Anna feels like she has been hitting badly and, though she knows it's wrong, she is upset right now not because of the shooting but because she's been moved in the lineup from second to sixth. If she keeps playing like this, Coach Jeff will start Becky at third base. Anna hates Becky because Becky has a long blond ponytail and wears mascara during practice. Worst of all, Anna is sure that Becky doesn't like her.

And all the girls on the Mt. Adams team feel that they would like to win this softball game. It makes them uncomfortable, this desire that doesn't go away. The three seniors who drive to Mar Vista together instead of riding in the bus are frank about it when they are alone in the car. *It isn't our fault*, they say to one another. *It isn't our fault that this happened.*

If we're going to play, they say, *then we have to play. I don't know what they want us to do about it.*

Certainly not throw the game, which would be as disrespectful as winning. *More disrespectful*, say the seniors, *because they suck at softball*. They tell one another how they are sure the girls of Mar Vista varsity softball are wonderful people, even if they are bad at softball.

Coach Jeff tosses whiffle balls to Lisa, whose swing is compact and powerful. She does not hold back just because it is practice. She cracks open one of the whiffle balls and it falls to the ground, spread open like a bird. *Another one*, says Coach, and she feels proud. She wants to break every whiffle ball in the world. Lisa loves being up to bat, the center of the entire game, feeling all of her power gather in her back leg and her loose hands, the barrel of her bat heavy but quick. She wants to be the one to drive the final run in, to hit the ball into the gap when there is a runner on second. This is why Anna is a bad hitter. Anyone can see it, Lisa always can, how Anna walks up to the batter's box like she's asking permission, like swinging at a bad pitch will kill her. Wrong word. Lisa wants to think about the game and nothing more. She wants to swing her bat and see the ball go so far so fast that it looks lazy in the sky, effortless. She will run around the bases like she owns them.

Coach Jeff hits sharp grounders to Becky who is never afraid of the ball but today flinches just enough to pull her glove out of the dirt, to let the ball sneak under.

Coach Jeff reminds himself that she may be upset, given the circumstances, but mostly he finds himself worried that they have a real weakness at third. Anna is getting worse and he's seen players go that way, more timid the more they play, each mistake adding up until their play is driven by fear. But Becky is usually fearless. It's a strange day, a sad day. He eases up a little on the grounders, lets them take a few hops before they reach her, and she brings them in cleanly, her face as it always is, inward and a little angry, the face of desire.

Becky is not afraid of the ball. Every girl on the team knows what a bruise from a ball looks like, a raised purple welt in the shape of an inner tube. When Becky was eight, her older brother died in a car accident. It's not a thing she tells people because it's a thing people never forget. She is surprised to find herself so distracted by the Mar Vista girls. She keeps looking over to them to see if they understand, as she does, that life is unfair. How could they not? And not even that, because unfair suggests a standard of fairness, something to hope for. Life is unrelated to such standards. Life is a physical activity achieved by the body—until it isn't anymore. Her body achieves a throw from third to first. She's got a big arm, Coach says. Big is, of course, the same as strong. Anna is right: Becky doesn't like her. Becky thinks that Anna feels she deserves to start because she has started in the past. But every game is a new game. One of these days, it'll be Becky, and when it is, she'll hold onto that spot for dear life. When she steps up to the plate, she will attack before she can be attacked.

The girls circle up. Coach Jeff says again that everyone on the field is a winner already. And then he says, *Molly, cheat left when number eight comes up. She's their best hitter. She pulls to center right.* When Coach Jeff leaves the huddle, the girls lock arms and realize they don't know what to do next. Usually they would scream and stomp, do the cheer they learned from the girls who went before them. *We're two games out of first,* the captain says. And then she doesn't say anything else. They kick at the dirt with cleats, they throw balls into the pockets of mitts. They are happy to have the captain's permission to do what they were going to do anyway.

Before the game begins, the teams line up on the baselines and take off their caps. It is a moment of silence. Lisa thinks about getting a hit and begins to pray for that but, abashed, instead thinks, *I'm sorry. I hope it's all okay. I know it isn't okay. I'm sorry.* Simone feels like she could cry but does not because that would be horrifying, attention seeking. Anna and Becky stand next to each other and feel at odds with each other and with themselves. Molly is dry-eyed and watching. She will grow up to be good in a moment of crisis but always a little distant, a little withheld, especially when she does not want to be. Molly is the first person to notice when a girl on the other team begins to cry. Not sloppily, but a few tears and then more, until the other girls on that team circle around her and hide her from view. The girls of Mt. Adams know, at this moment, that something real and horrible and true has happened, something that cannot be changed or even understood, and the right fielder and left fielder grasp hands, and the left fielder holds hands with Simone who holds hands with Lisa, and on down the line, in a gesture that relieves the adults, so respectful and thoughtful, but the girls are doing it for themselves, to feel a part of something, not a part of this tragedy, which is not theirs to own, but a part of their team on this particular day, a piece of something larger than themselves. They look across the dirt to the girl who has seen what they are afraid they will someday have to see, and in the face of this crying girl, winning seems wrong, and losing seems wrong, and playing seems wrong when the world around the game is so real.

And then the game begins. Up to bat first, the girls of Mt. Adams are clumsy. With none of the usual chatter and cheering from the dugout, they feel alone at the plate. The crack of the bat on the ball is loud as it ricochets foul. The girl with the tear-stained face crouches at second and Anna swings at bad pitches. She has never been so eager to be invisible. When the third out is called—Anna hits a weak grounder to the shortstop—they all feel relief, and shame. Coach Jeff says nothing. Mitts on, they jog onto the field like they've been taught, *you don't walk, you run*, crossing the sharp chalk lines, spreading out across the smooth dirt and the grass that is so even and green. Taking their positions as the pitcher takes the mound, they adjust their hats. They wait, crouched, bouncing lightly on the balls of their feet.

When the pitcher releases the ball, they follow it from the hand to the bat, and then the ball is in play and they are in motion. They stay low though the ball comes in fast, wait until they feel the ball in their mitts before they rise, and even as they rise, they are pulling the ball from the glove. Anna and Lisa and Molly and Becky don't know how to grip a ball without rotating it in their palms, without picking out a seam for the thumb, a seam for the middle three fingers. A whip of the arm sends the ball flying. Simone reaches out, stretches her body, back foot firm on first base, ready to feel the ball meet her mitt with a sharp pop. The first out is called. Then, as they always do, they throw the ball around the horn, everyone getting their chance, staying warm, holding hands across an empty space.

Simone gets the ball back, circle complete. She feels the pleasant sting in her hand, the sting that means she's alive. She slaps her closed mitt against her leg, calls *one down, two to go*, and flicks the ball back to the pitcher.

FRIDAY NIGHT

My husband and I should be making a baby but instead we argue about whether to go out for Mexican or order pizza, each taking our standard positions: he likes the neighborhood Mexican place, damning it as *good enough*, and me, I know the Mexican place is fine but good enough is not enough when we could get mediocre pizza at home and, while we're waiting, oh, that's right, I'm ovulating, let's go; I take off my bra to show I mean business but he puts on a shoe because lately my husband needs to be in the *mood*, he needs to feel like sex is about *love* and *us* and *not just about knocking me up*—to which I say, what, is meaningless sex not hot anymore?, and I know knocking women up is a fetish, I've been on Reddit, so imagine me swelling and ripening and bursting with seed like a rotten melon thrown across a field by a trebuchet, spilling its guts across the grass, or whatever, I'm not here to tell anyone how to get their dick hard, but I do know I'm losing wood while my husband sits on the couch, one shoe off, one shoe one, saying that we should get out more, to which I say the Mexican restaurant down the street doesn't count as "getting out more" and you know what, you know what, you only want to go out because you don't want to fuck me and he says that isn't true but also do I have to put it like that? and this is when I lose it because it isn't as though sex has always been about *love*, about *us*, about anything other than getting my husband's rocks off, so I wave his other shoe at him and I say, now it's your turn to suck it up like a big girl, and he says, how the fuck am I supposed to get a boner when I'm sucking it up like a big girl and I say, imagine I'm someone else, obviously, like, do you even know what sex *is*?, and that is apparently unacceptable even though, as I said, my egg is on the fucking move like Wile E. Coyote ten feet past the edge of the cliff, gravity about to ruin his day, and my husband leaves the room and slams the door and I can hear him say *goddamit*, I can hear him get on the phone and order the pizza, a veggie garden delight, and he doesn't ask to add pepperonis on half because he knows that I love pepperonis and he's pissed off, pissed off enough to do something petty, something petty that when the pizza arrives there will be no hiding from, and when he finally comes back into the room I don't tell him that I heard; he sits beside me on the bed and takes my hand and it seems he's knocked the wind out of himself and we bump shoulders and even as I wonder what we're doing, how we can be allowed to make a baby when we don't qualify for a loan, when we buy our wine from the pharmacy, when we fight, and buy clever T-shirts online that we don't need and can't afford, when I am medicated for depression and he is a chronic nose picker, yes, even as I think that we are barely clinging to the scab that covers the molten earth, my husband presses me onto my back on our IKEA bed with one leg propped up by books and kisses my face and then my breasts and it isn't erotic but it is sweet and his body is heavy on top of me and, bless him, he is getting his dick hard, thinking about strangers: women who wear latex and pop balloons, and he pushes inside me and in an hour the pizza will arrive, and we'll open the box and inside, look, there's the pizza with no pepperonis and god, whatever we make together, if we make anything together, when we open the box there's no promise that there will even be pepperonis *or* vegetables, it could be a BBQ chicken pizza, which neither of us like, or a wet mess of Thai noodles, or a fish, dead eyes and cold scales, and why do I want my husband to hold me down on this bed while we wait for the pizza without pepperonis, while he pretends I am someone else and screws his eyes shut and screws into me but this is what we are doing and he comes with a whimper and holds me and whispers *I love you* against my hair in that way he always has, and when he leaves to clean himself up I know he's thinking about the pizza with no pepperonis, wishing he hadn't done that, hoping we can laugh it off, as if I don't know that the pizza is in the oven, is on its way, as if, when it arrives, I'll do anything other than eat it, because I often need forgiveness, because I love him, and so when we open that box I'll roll my eyes at him, smile, but I won't say anything more, won't spoil our dinner with talk about the absence of the pepperoni, about the empty space inside of me that insists, without ceasing or reason, to be filled, whether we are ready, whether I am ready, or not.

HERE PREACHED HIS LAST

The first time I see the ghost of George Whitefield, I'm fucking my neighbor Karl. We're going at it with more enthusiasm than finesse, the way you do when things are new. I lift my head, I'm going to kiss or perhaps bite Karl's neck, and that's when I see him: George, sitting at the end of the bed in knickers, vest, and long coat, hair tied back in a queue. *Whore*, the ghost whispers, and damn, he knows what gets me off. *Whore whore whore*. I come so hard I get a foot cramp and Karl says *fuck yeah*. He can't see George. Karl lacks imagination. It's one of his best qualities.

I've never seen a ghost before, but then I've never had an affair before either. Karl and I have known each other for a few years—I teach English at the academy, he teaches physics. Karl's handsome of course and we'd drunkenly made out once, ages ago, after a faculty party, stupid and sloppy like the teenagers we teach. Neither of us ever brought it up again. When we finally have sex, it's because I ask him to come up to my apartment. I'm going to lend him a book. I stand by the bookshelf, he stands by the bed, and then I move to him and we're on each other. Now, Karl is lying on my breast, breathing hard, while George Whitefield looks slightly up and away from our tangle, reminding us that though we've forgotten our modesty, he has not. Outside, the academy kids are hurrying down the sidewalks to their dorms, hunched into the cold wind. I run a finger down Karl's belly. I'm less lonely than I've been in a long time, warm inside with a lover, a ghost, and a secret to keep me company. And I don't mean the affair, though that's a secret too. No, the secret I've just learned is that I can fuck without caring for the other person at all.

The fucking seems momentous, the beginning of an adventure, and at first I'm in a bit of a fog: horny, guilty, and proud. *Whore*, George says every day when I leave and again when I come home. He's perched atop his stone marker in the strip of grass between the road and the sidewalk outside my house. It reads: *George White-field Here Preached His Last Sermon, September 29, 1770.* Moss grows in the letters and the snow almost buries it. I like to blow George a kiss, which makes him scowl. For a few glorious months, I feel like I'm getting away with something, fucking Karl and still living my boring life. *Do you have to call it fucking?* Karl will sometimes ask and I say, *Isn't the fact that it's fucking what makes it fun?* Sometimes he laughs. Every so often, though, he rolls his eyes and looks away instead, like I've hurt his feelings, and I have to coax him into feeling better, which I hate. *Are you okay? What's wrong?* Karl says nothing's wrong, but do I have to be so crass?

Karl, I think, doesn't like to be reminded that we're doing a bad thing for no other reason than it feels good.

"I'm sorry," I say to him even though I'm not, and before he distracts me with a kiss, I wonder why I'm risking so much just to have another person to apologize to.

When I'm not teaching, coaching the varsity soccer team, or having an affair, I am busy worrying about my daughter Emmy. She is six, and so happy I think it can only be a bad sign. She loves pink and princesses, which

I was prepared for, but she also makes friends easily and never seems to bully or be bullied. I don't see myself in her, which is good, but now I fear that a happy, well-adjusted child will be even more wounded by the world than an anxious, angry child with a large gap between her two front teeth. My daughter does not know what it is to hesitate. When she comes home from school, she throws herself into my arms. When she gets out of the car in the morning, she throws herself into the playground, scattering her classmates like crows. At swimming lessons, she doesn't notice that the water is different than the air—she leaps. My husband tells me that I am literally making trouble out of happiness. I tell him he's a man and doesn't know any better and then we fight. My best friend, Suze, agrees with me, of course. She knows the world is hard for girls who haven't learned to be cautious.

The varsity soccer team is the opposite of my daughter. They seem to do nothing but hesitate. *You're never going to win a header by asking permission*, I tell them. But they refuse to attack the ball. They'd rather lose than look like they're trying to win. It's a feeling I remember, though as a teenager I preempted failure in different ways. Baggy shirts, scuffed sneakers, thick black eyeliner, a belly-button piercing. I didn't know if I wanted boys to look at me—men had already been looking for a while—and so I made sure if they did look they'd see a girl who didn't give a shit. The belly-button piercing got so infected after a month that I had to tell my mother, who instead of being furious with me was just exasperated. Ten days of antibiotics and a scar that, when I was pregnant with Emmy, stretched in an angry twist away from my navel. I liked to trace it with my finger and wonder what scars my baby would get some-day. Ones, I hoped, with better stories behind them.

I yell at the girls on the field that they better start hustling or we'll be doing extra sprints at the end of practice. I loved playing soccer in high school, running until I was about to collapse, letting the work of it hol-low me out.

"Shoot the ball!" I yell as the center forward passes to her teammate even with a clear shot on the open net.

The center forward kicks the grass with her cleat and looks at her watch. *We're running over*, she's telling me.

Practice goes long. Then I meet with three students about their papers. Then I answer a series of emails all from the same parent. Emmy and I eat macaroni and cheese with chopped up hotdog. Emmy takes forever to go to sleep, excited that tomorrow her class gets to visit Mr. Lettuce, the school guinea pig. I get in bed beside her and read her favorite book, about a little girl mouse who writes all her wishes on pieces of paper and plants them in the garden. When the little girl mouse wakes up the next day, the garden is bursting with strange plants: polka dot flowers, a tree that reaches to the clouds, a fly trap so big it could eat little girl mouse in one bite. *Noomf!* I say, and my hand bites Emmy's arm. One day, the little girl mouse plants a wish for a best friend and the next morning she finds an egg. When she breaks it open, a bright red bird cries out and flies away, to the top of a hill, then a mountain. The little girl mouse plants wishes on her journey, so that when she finds the bird, they can both go home. I read the book to Emmy twice before she admits that she's sleepy. Before she drifts off she asks if tomorrow we can plant some of her wishes.

My husband is not here to help with this. He's gone a lot, helping companies whose workflows aren't flowing. Right now he's in Japan. At least I have George, who sits with me in the kitchen. He's decent company. A little doom and gloom, but he likes to laugh.

"We're going to get creamed by Valley City High on Saturday," I tell George. I pour a glass of wine and pull out a stack of papers to grade, the gesture entirely symbolic. I take a deep drink.

You are an adulteress who is destined for hellfire, George responds. *But fear not. I reside in heaven and, for all its beauties, its holy ecstasies, it is not everything which man has promised.*

"Is that right?" I ask. He laughs and laughs.

No, he says. *Do not be absurd. And Hell is not the way you imagine it. The ways of Satan are more subtle, more inventive.*

"Really?" I ask.

No. He does not laugh. *There is no need for subtlety. Only foolish sinners like you imagine there is something worse than pain.*

I pour myself another glass of wine.

"It's a big game," I say. "We need to win it if we want a chance at the playoffs."

George doesn't respond. He seems to have lost steam and reverts to the tried and true. *Whore whore whore*, he whispers, and I keep drinking, more than I should on a Wednesday night, or any night, and eventually he switches to *glutton glutton glutton.*

Next afternoon, I'm in a hurry, late to get Emmy from afterschool care. Spring is mud season in New Hampshire, and I pick my way across campus, avoiding the puddles that have formed in the sidewalk's depressions. It surprises me every year, how the melted snow discovers this hidden topography, everything flat revealed to be craggy. I'm almost there when I get a text from Karl. you free for a faculty meeting tonight? Karl's wife is *not* in Japan and he worries a lot about his wife seeing our messages. busy with emmy, I reply, and usually I'd send a little something else, a *sorry* or a *let's reschedule the meeting*, with an emoji that is friendly without being obviously sexual, an ear of corn or a fireman, but in the brief moment that my typing distracts me I step ankle deep into a small lake. The water is so cold I feel the bite before I realize I'm wet through my shoes and my socks. My first impulse is to swear but I laugh instead and put my phone away. I am a woman who lacks the sense to watch where she's going. When I pick up Emmy, I tell her I've been playing in puddles and I offer to carry her on my back while I do it again. I tell her that since my shoes are already wet, it doesn't matter if I get them a bit wetter, but we have to make sure her feet stay warm. We splash and splash until my jeans are soaked too and shiver our way home.

Thursday night is Spring Fling! at Emmy's elementary school and I am in charge of making her costume. Her grade is performing "Twist and Shout" and I've sewn together a pink poodle skirt, the kind I would have killed for when I was six. Emmy stands on a box for fitting. The hem is crooked and the poodle's eye is weeping with dried super glue like it's infected.

"You look great," I say. Emmy does a twirl. I wonder if she is too young to see the flaws. The other mothers will certainly notice. The other little girls will too.

My pocket vibrates. Karl has texted me again. **we need to talk**, he says.

everything ok?? I ask.

having some thoughts on faculty meeting

I tell him I'll see him tomorrow after his class.

Emmy is twisting hard in her skirt, jumping up and down, and then she's fallen over and she's crying. A pin holding the hem of the skirt has stabbed her leg.

"Look, baby," I say, and I hold up the skirt to show her the smallest dot of blood on her skin. "You're okay." The poodle gazes at me, sick and hateful.

My pocket vibrates again, Emmy has stopped crying and is inspecting the blood now, blotting it with the tip of her finger, about to get it on the skirt, which is the last thing that skirt needs, and I am *done* with Karl, I swear, I am already writing him the message that ends everything when I see that the text is from my husband instead. It's very early in the morning, too early for him to be awake, but he can't sleep. He says he misses me. He says the cherry blossoms will bloom soon, but he'll be home just before they do. Figures, he texts, and adds a smiley face, as if to say, oh this wild dance we call life, what can you do, and right about now, as I try to remember if Emmy has white tights with no holes, as she yanks on the hem of the dress and I wait for the howl that says she's stabbed herself again, I hate him.

When I get to the kitchen, George is there. My eyes are red and I've stabbed my own fingers on the skirt's pins too many times to count, too many times for what is still an ugly, hopeless thing. George shakes his head and says, *These are the wages of sin*, and I throw my wine into his face and it passes right through him, stains my perfectly nice kitchen chair, surprises us both.

"Shit," I say, and grab a roll of paper towels, yanking off sheets and pressing them through George's body, and though of course we can't touch and he tries to pretend he cannot see me (oh George, I know your looks now, how you gaze into the middle distance when you aren't comfortable with what's happening right before your eyes), I can sense him squirm. I slow down just a little, patting the seat dry gently and thoroughly. The wine has stained the cheap wicker. I'm kneeling in front of George, the mess absorbed into a dripping clot of paper towels. I wonder, whore that I am, if he ever had a woman on her knees in front of him. I want to ask but, I admit, I'm afraid. I'm afraid I'd ask and when he said no, offer to suck his cock. I get up, throw the paper towels away, and pour myself another glass of wine. I sit primly and say, "I forgive you."

And the best thing happens. George smiles, which I've never seen before. It's short lived and after he calls me *whore* with such enthusiasm that I know he means it but I also know he wishes he didn't like me.

"Have you ever been in love?" I ask, which is not the question I had wanted to ask, but maybe in George's time love and a blowjob had been one and the same.

George does not answer.

"I have," I say, which is obvious. I'm married, aren't I? But I think married people aren't given enough credit for being in love. For being in love with each other— which everyone treats as a given, as mandatory, which is the *hardest* way to love—but also for remembering what it's like to be in love with someone else, for know-ing that every love is different and sticking with the love you have. Of course I've loved other men. That boy in Introduction to Astronomy who had sex with me in my dorm room—we'd been studying the names of star clusters—and then told me he had a long-distance girl-friend. A man who restored furniture and cooked elab-orate meals for me. I could think of no greater sign of devotion. I moved to New Mexico with him for three months and for the last month he refused to touch me, called it a religious practice, but eventually confessed he had gotten chlamydia from another woman. Eventually my husband, who I do love, even though some days that love is hard to find.

I don't say all of this to George. Good old George, who sits on his stone and watches the academy kids walk by, the small dogs in sweaters, the old couples who lean close but still can't hear each other. George feels Jesus' love for all of them, but no sympathy for me. At this point I'm a little drunk and edging dangerously close to self-pity.

It is love which brings man closest to God, George says.

"Thank you, George," I say, and I'm so surprised by his kindness that I almost cry.

Love and sincere repentance.

"Okay, George," I say. "I get it."

When I get to his class, Karl is at the whiteboard, spray-ing then rubbing at the traces of past lessons. He looks good, better looking and a little younger than me. His wife is better looking than me too. The two of them go hiking and cross-country skiing on the weekends. Though we've had sex many times, I am often struck with the improbability of it. Why bother with fucking me? I shut the classroom door behind me, ready for him to break up with me, assuming he will and hoping for it. I'd break up with him but I don't have the energy. I'm thinking about whether I put Emmy's dance shoes in her bag for the show tonight.

"I have to tell my wife about us," Karl says. He puts down the whiteboard eraser, runs his hand through his hair.

"What's happened?" I ask, but I already know.

"I have to tell her how I feel," he says.

"You don't have to do anything," I say.

"She deserves to know."

"We can stop seeing each other."

"It isn't fair to her."

"We have to stop seeing each other."

"I know you feel the same way I do." Karl takes my hand in his and presses a tender kiss to my knuckles, something he has never done before. I yank my hand away. *This is absurd*, I want to say. *We don't feel any-thing.* And as I clutch my hand to my chest, I imagine my mother in the audience, shaking her head at this mess, saying, *sweetie, you always did make life harder for yourself.*

George Whitefield sits beside her. *Good madam,* he says, *this is why I turned away from the passions of the stage to become a preacher. Your daughter is already a fornicator and a sinner. All this pageantry will not save her immortal soul.*

"She knows about us," I say.

"No," he says. "She suspects."

He backs me up against the desk, angry, a little scary. I'm afraid but also turned on and confused, because I've never had the kind of sex we're about to have. He lifts me up onto the desk, pulls my underwear down, and then we're fucking and he's not even trying to get me off. I look over his shoulder at the periodic table. Karl is a good teacher. He knows a lot about baseball and loves football but doesn't watch anymore because he thinks it's morally wrong. He has a scar on his arm from where a small tumor was removed and sometimes I feel an urge to touch it, as if scars are where we're most vulnerable and not the thickened skin where we feel the least.

After he comes, he holds me, murmurs in my ear that he's sorry, that he loves me. He's confused me, what we just did, for someone and something else.

"I don't love you," I say. He flinches. "Don't do something you can't take back."

"We've already done that," he says.

"You don't love me," I say, but he insists he does. As I said, he lacks imagination, and so he imagines that love is the only excuse for what we've done.

Oh, Karl, I think. You're an idiot.

I want to go home and pass out and forget that I'm a wife and a mother and a lover and a teacher but it's Spring Fling! so I put on fresh deodorant and get my daughter into her costume. She wiggles with so much excitement while I put it on her that the zipper breaks *again* and Jesus *fucking* Christ I feel my cell phone vibrate and I bet it's fucking Karl and I have one of those moments where I think I'm going to lose it. But I don't lose it because I can't. I safety pin my daughter into her skirt and say, "Hope that holds, munchkin."

I brush her fine hair into a pony tail. Other mothers will have made better skirts and done fancier hairdos.

Other mothers aren't fucking the science teacher either, I think, and sigh. George Whitefield leans against the wall as I work, no help at all, and when my daughter is out of the room I tell him to not even start with me. A horn honks outside and there's Suze, who has a son in the same grade. We choose seats in the back of the auditorium like delinquents and watch the kids perform.

My daughter's poodle skirt stays on and she's front and center and happy to be there. Suze's son is in the back row of kids and his hair is gelled into a helmet. He doesn't twist much but boy, oh, boy the kid can shout.

Suze knows about Karl but not about the ghost of George Whitefield.

After the show, while the teachers are talking to their classes, I show Suze Karl's latest texts:

> *still thinking about what happened*
>
> *don't think you meant to be hurtful*
>
> *i have to do what i think is right*

Suze has never approved of me fucking Karl, but she doesn't say I told you so.

"If I were you," she says, "I'd say you were lying, that you do love him too. That way, he'll say it's too much pressure and realize he doesn't love you after all."

Suze says that this has worked on countless of her past boyfriends.

I wonder what I can do to hurt Karl so badly he'll never think of loving me again. I try to remember who I've alienated and how. A girl in fourth grade was my friend until I realized that no one else liked her. So I told the girl she smelled weird and stopped eating lunch with her. I had a boyfriend who said I never opened up to him, which wasn't true. I'd told him everything there was to know about me; it just turned out that there wasn't much to know. So I started to make up things to confess until he left me because I was too much of a burden. My childhood cat never liked me. She pissed in my room.

"Maybe I can wait him out," I say, and Suze shakes her head. "He's a man," she says and leaves it at that.

I take my daughter for ice cream as a special treat for doing such a great job twisting and shouting. Mint chip for me, bubble gum with chunks of real blue bubble gum for her. We sit outside even though it's a little too cold, our sweaters pushed up our arms because our cones are dripping. She sees a spider and she tries to feed it ice cream. She dabs the melted drips in the spider's path. The spider walks around the ice cream. I tell her that some spiders are picky. "For that spider," I say, "ice cream could be like pickles." My daughter hates pickles. "Pickle ice cream!" she giggles and she wipes her hand against the poodle skirt and the poodle's eye comes away on her sticky finger. She gazes at the eye, jiggles it to watch the pupil dance.

"I'm going to plant this," she says. "It's a wish." Emmy screws her eyes shut and thinks hard. I want to ask what she's wished for, but I don't. I know wishes are sacred and secret. I've taught her that. And I think for the first time that that's a mistake. Why, of everything we think, should our wishes be unspoken?

"Now you too," she says, and hands me a piece of bubble gum from her melted ice cream.

I would like to plant a wish and watch it grow, but right now I don't know what to ask for. I suppose I should wish that I'd never had sex with Karl. I would like to wish that, but I can't. I don't regret cheating on my husband, even now. Instead I regret other things. I regret that it took me this long to learn to use my body for its own sake, to let my only emotion during sex be lust, be greed. I don't know what to do with this information, wasted as it seemed on my forties, on my marriage. I did not expect my affair to make me so angry. I regret that my husband is a good man but far away.

Sometimes, I wish I could tell my daughter about all this. Not now, of course, but when she's older. I want to tell her, sweetheart, before you get married, have casual sex and remember: nothing matters.

I suppose that sounds bleak. I suppose that's not what I mean.

And remember: be selfish.

I plant the bubble gum as deep as I can and pat the dirt down over it.

Emmy smiles and I lick my finger and dab her cheeks as she tries to wriggle away. Her ponytail is half fallen out, the poodle skirt filthy. My phone buzzes in my pocket. She sees a friend of hers and runs over to her, and the other mom waves at me like we're confirming a prisoner transfer.

Karl texts again. Each buzz is aggressive.

meet me tmr at soccer practice, I text to him, just to make it stop.

"Maybe I'll become a nun," I say to George.

After this, George says, *no man will cleave to you. Including God.* He laughs and laughs. *Whore,* he chuckles.

"Whore," I agree.

George has never asked me why I fuck Karl. To him, there are no degrees of wrong, there is simply the wrong itself. There are no degrees of repentance, only absolute abasement, and I have failed. I think George likes that I never try to explain my actions to him. But I've explained them to myself. Justified them, I suppose. Here is what I think. Every day I wake up. I shower but I don't pay much attention to how it feels. I eat what I always eat and I chew my bite of toast as I chase my daughter around, and button her up, and feed her too, and I couldn't tell you what the bread tastes like. Half the time I've burned it. I go to work and I use my mind and sometimes my students use my mind and other times they let their minds wander and it is just my mind and their bodies in the room. I would love for them to see the beautiful poem or passage I'm showing them, I'm straining at them with love for it, but they aren't there. I go home and take care of my daughter, who is all body, and I strain with love for her and talk to her father on the phone and miss him some but not enough because I am so angry that he has left me here all alone and at night I am finally, finally, truly alone and I drink a glass of wine or three, anything to put my mind to sleep, to knock myself unconscious for as long as I can before it starts all over again.

Why would I not fuck Karl?

Soccer practice isn't going well. It's cold for late March and though it's above freezing, the sky is somehow spitting flecks of snow. The game is tomorrow and the girls are scrimmaging, ten on ten, no goalies. They're supposed to be taking it easy but also focusing on keeping wide, keeping the field open, creating space for opportunities.

"Amanda," I shout, "You are the *left* wing, *left*!" I wave my arm and she moves slowly back toward the far side. "Do you not see Rachel open at the post?" I yell, when, instead of crossing the ball, my midfielder dribbles straight into a clump of defenders.

I blow my whistle. The girls jog over, gather up. I tell them that since they don't seem interested in playing, we're going to run sprints instead. I shouldn't do this. They need their legs fresh for tomorrow. Karl hasn't arrived yet.

I send them to the goal post and back. Fence and back. The tall bush at the end of the field and back and every girl has to bring me a leaf or, if there aren't enough new leaves, a twig. When one doesn't hand over anything, I make them run it again. I know how they are feeling, I remember it—legs limp, mind empty, pushed to the edge of what I could endure. It had felt good when I was young, to be run like an animal. The leaf trick—my own high school coach used that. I think it was meant to show us that we were all in it together, that if one of us tried to cheat we would all be let down. But that wasn't the lesson I'd learned from it. I'd learned that people cheated even when they knew they'd be caught. That sometimes getting caught is a form of defiance.

"Again," I say, and on the run back one girl falls to her knees and throws up. Number twelve kneels next to her, holds her ponytail out of the way, pats her back until the girl is done. These girls who don't play as a team all look at me with the same expression of loathing and I realize that I hate them too, a little, for not loving the same thing I did.

I say, "Okay, girls." Practice is over.

I turn to start putting the equipment back in the bag and there is Karl. I don't know how long he's been watching but it's long enough. It is easy to read his face. Disgust at first, at the vomit, at me turning away instead of moving toward the girl on the ground, as I should. Disbelief, briefly, and then every other emotion is chased away by anger, like I've tricked him, made him believe I was someone else.

He holds my gaze for a few moments and then turns and walks away. No need for me to say anything more. I am bad enough, exactly as I am, and I wish George were there to simply say it aloud, to comfort me with his honesty.

That night, George isn't at my kitchen table, though I sit and wait for him. Eventually, I go upstairs and fall asleep atop the covers, still dressed, and when I wake, it's a little after two in the morning. My phone says I have eighteen text messages from an unknown number and after seeing the first one, you fucked my husband—straight to the point—I turn my phone off. The street-light is shining in my window and when I go to close the curtain, I see George, standing beside his stone as if waiting for something. In the kitchen he usually looks solid, though he seems to hover rather that sit. Right now, though, he looks spectral, emitting an almost pagan blue glow. I put on my coat and go out into the street.

It is snowing in earnest now, drifting sideways across the streetlights, landing in my hair, sticking to the flower stalks that have misjudged the arrival of spring. George doesn't notice me. There is no trace of contempt on his face, only anticipation. He paces a little, directs unseen spectators to give him more room and I realize I know what he's preparing for. I've researched George, of course. Went to the library and read about the ghost who sat outside my house, who kept me company. He came to this town to preach in the town hall but when he got here there were far too many people, thousands too many, and so even though he was very sick, he decided to preach outside. George loved to preach outside. Outside there was room for everyone. Room even for me. He placed a wooden board across two barrels, right at this spot where the granite marker is, so that people could see him. It is cold and my toes are getting numb in my slippers but I have to stay. George is about to preach his last sermon.

I can't see the hand that George takes to help him up onto the stone. Every time he coughs, his body shakes like his soul is trying to rip free. He raises his hands for silence and waits several beats, his face fierce. When he begins to speak, I can't hear him. I clench my jaw to keep my teeth from chattering. His right hand slices wide, his eyes flash. He coughs. At times, he pauses, as if unsure he'll go on, but then he does, more frantically than before, gesticulating, serious one moment, then smiling the next as if he can see the Lord before him, is conjuring him here for the assembled to see. He is so sure of himself. Oh, George. You know, don't you, that those thousands of ears are like cracked bowls, like the ears of my students, my daughter. You fill them, yes, George, but most of what you say leaks out onto the wet earth and disappears. Not everything, though, I suppose. Someone remembered to plant this stone.

I know that when George is done, the story will change. I will go upstairs and read those text messages. I will face my colleagues, who will all know what I've done. My husband will come home, just before those cherry blossoms bloom. Everything will become messy. But right now, the story isn't about him. The story is about me, and I watch George preach until he can barely stand, until I can't feel my fingers. When he finally gets down from the stone, he turns to a man I cannot see and shakes his hand. He turns to another and claps him on the back, puts a hand to his own powdered wig to steady it. His step is slow and tired through the invisible crowd. He has a word for everyone, and though I can't hear what he says to the others, though he leaves me farther behind every moment, in my ear I can still hear him whisper joyfully *whore whore whore*.

And I say *yes yes yes*. Yes, I'm here, I'm here, a body, just a body, and it's not promised to anyone, it's mine, only mine, and I miss that, God, oh God, oh George, I miss it.

FIRST WOMAN HANGED
FOR WITCHCRAFT IN
WALES, 1594

Nursing is women's work, so it comes as no surprise when they hang me for it. *You should've stuck to weaving, Gwen*, Mother tells me before they pull the trap.

There are many ways to heal.

For a cut, mix lye soap and sugar. Rub it into the wound, bind the wound with cloth, and in a day, check that the remedy has pushed dirt from the flesh. If the edges of the cut become red, if there is pus or fever, grind calendula and lavender and pack the wound again.

For boils, prepare a poultice of crushed garlic. For boils on a man who beats his wife, prepare a poultice of crushed garlic and sheep urine. The sheep urine will not make the poultice ineffective, but it will increase both his sensory discomfort and your personal satisfaction. Do not tell the wife what you have done. She does not need the burden. Do not tell Mother, either. She already looks at you like you are a dangling thread she thought she had snipped.

When Mother's back aches from bending over her loom, she will tell you to be quiet. Sometimes she will hit you. Sometimes she will let you put ground mint against her temples and if she closes her eyes, she will tell you a story.

I am five when Mother first tells me the story of the afanc.

In a deep lake beside a small village, lived a creature part beaver, part crocodile, as big as a fat pony.

Take me to the lake! I cry.

That's not really how this works, Mother says.

I am eight when a neighboring family gives Mother a lamb in exchange for her weaving. The lamb is clumsy and grows into a clumsy sheep. *Get that sheep out of that ditch, Gwen.* But everyone knows that sheep love ditches and, even more than grass or sweets, they love being difficult. My sheep and I stay at the bottom of the ditch and watch the weather blow by. *That sheep is not a pet, Gwen.* But what is a pet except an animal you lay your hands on?

The afanc caused horrible flooding. With a sweep of its beaver tail, it broke down dams and ruined fields. But when villagers came to kill it, it snapped its crocodile jaws and sank quickly away.

One day, the town decided that a virgin could lure the afanc from the waters.

Why? I asked.

Magical creatures cannot resist virgins.

Why? I asked.

Because, Mother says, and sits me back down to my mending. Her hands fly across her loom.

Because virgins smell like summer even in the cold. Because when they walk, they forget where they are for minutes at a time. Because when they wake, they are pleased to greet the morning. Because when they look at something ugly, they see the something and forgive the ugly.

Already I am making the story my own.

I am twelve when Father returns home for the last time. He sails the coast, staying home only for the worst of winter. When he leaves every spring, he gives me a wooden carving and Mother a baby.

All my sisters die before they can be born.

For a swollen, milk-full breast, apply cow dung. Or the large leaves of the foxglove. Or let a puppy suckle. *Get that dog away from my tits, Gwen.* It is a relief when winter returns and Father does not. If I could be a sailor, I would never return either. I would have a tattoo of a mermaid on my upper breast and stand on deck until my cheeks were brown and my hands rough with rope burn.

Without sisters, I weave daisy crowns and lay them on my sheep's indifferent ears.

What happens to the virgin? I ask, but mother is too exhausted for distraction. I do most of the weaving now.

Her hands ache when she eats and when she sleeps. When her courses come, she bleeds too much for too long. She dreams of ice.

You tell me, she says.

There are many ways to heal.

For a small scrape, tell a story about a journey. For a wasting disease, tell a long story, a story in which good triumphs, to pass the time. When you spin a story out, read your listener's face. She will tell you when to press, when to relieve the pressure.

But Mother never likes the way I tell stories.

Once the villagers agreed that they needed a virgin, they chose a girl who was pretty but not the prettiest. They did not want to waste their best virgin. Virgin, *they said,* go down to the water tomorrow at sunrise and sing to the afanc. Once you've lured it from the water, we will swoop in and kill it. *The virgin was afraid. She tried to find a man who would have sex with her.* Please, *she said.* This hymen is doing me no good at all.

The first man the virgin approached said no, and ran away, afraid of the other villagers. The second man said no, and ran away, ashamed of himself. The third man said yes, and took her to his home, and locked her inside. He was sick of his fields flooding, he was hungry, and the virgin was not his type anyway. Before the sun rose, the third man led the virgin to the water's edge, and then ran back behind the trees with the others. The virgin sang a little, but her voice was thin and she was very afraid. Instead she whispered to the afanc. Please, Mr. Afanc, *she said,* please stay in the water. They're going to try to kill you.

At this, the water bubbled with the afanc's laughter. He raised his crocodile face above the surface and said, They cannot hurt me with their spears.

I thought not, *said the virgin.* If you stay put, I'm sure they'll give up soon and then you won't need to eat me.

The afanc preferred to eat fish, but he sometimes ate a villager's hand, just for show. Flooding the village was so easy he'd grown bored. He was lonely.

I will stay in the water, *said the afanc,* but you must promise me that you'll return at midnight every night for a week, to talk with me. *And when she nodded, he turned his head away and disappeared back out into the lake.*

The virgin was also bored and lonely. The village was not a very fun place because everyone was starving or dying in childbirth. Every night for the next week, she went down to the edge of the water and spoke with the afanc, and every night, the third man followed and watched her speak, though he could not hear her. He hadn't been that attracted to her before, but once she put the idea in his head, it began to grow. On the sixth day, he spoke to her father and got her hand in marriage. On the sixth night, the afanc noticed she was sad.

This is the last time we will ever talk, *she said.* Tomorrow I have to get married, and then I'll no longer be a virgin.

Why do I care if you're a virgin? *asked the afanc.* You people are obsessed with hymens. What matters to me is that you're blond.

The virgin realized that this was a joke and it made her cry. She did not want to get married. The third man was not funny and had locked her in his house. The afanc said, Come with me, then. I will drown you in the lake, pull you through the hole in the bottom of the world, and when you wake, we will both be afanc. We will live in a much better lake than this one. Your lake, frankly, is the pits.

The virgin thought about the afanc's offer and about her wedding and the many babies she would have to bear. She thought about her father, who was looking forward to receiving a goat in exchange for her, and though she hated to disappoint him, she stood and walked out into the lake. The third man ran from behind the tree, begging her not to sacrifice herself, but she did not listen. Her white nightdress ballooned in the water and glowed in the moonlight. The afanc wrapped her blond hair in his snout and pulled her under, never to return.

The third man told the villagers about the virgin's sacrifice. They gave her father three goats and congratulated themselves on a job well done. Hymens were, as they'd suspected, terrifically important. The third man mourned for a short while and then married a different girl, who died the next winter with a son in her arms.

Do you think the afanc was telling the truth? my sheep asks.

Why bother killing her if he didn't love her? I say.

There are many ways to heal, and some do use magic.

Pick the tufts of wool that a sheep you love leaves on thorns. Sew the tufts into a pouch and keep it in your pocket.

Scrape the salt from your father's coat as it dries by the fire. Take some of the salt, and sprinkle it on a fresh cooked fish. The fish will taste delicious and you will remember the location of something you've lost. Take the rest of the salt, and sew it into a pouch and wear the pouch around your neck.

Do not leave a crown of daisies to wilt on the ground. Keep the daisies and sew them into the hems of your skirts. The daisies will whisper when someone wishes you harm.

I am seventeen when the sheep of the village start dying. They are found on their sides, with bloated tongues and bloated bellies.

The villagers do not like that I put sheep urine in their poultices. They do not like the looks I give their handsome sons. They do not like the stories I tell their children. They do not like that my sheep is fat and healthy. When the villagers arrive at my house, they take my sheep. They slaughter her and gather her blood in a deep bowl. With the blood, they paint their lintels and their palms. With the body, they make tough roasts. I promise them they will regret it.

A farmer's son cuts himself on a rock. I pack his cut with lye soap and sugar. The next day, the skin is hot and red. I pack the cut with calendula and lavender. Pus seeps from the cut. I tell the child the story of the red dragon of Dinas Emrys. How the dragon loved his mountain and how he loved a boy who would someday be a great wizard.

When the child dies, the farmer swears I cursed him. *Gwen Ferch Ellis*, he whispers. Or yells. Or feels in his nails. I am not present for the moment the father finds the name for his grief.

As the door drops out from under me, I ask the wool and salt and daisies to speak to the air on my behalf. The air whispers to the earth and the earth refuses to pull me to it. The men watch with mouths open, the women with eyes open. I have always been full of things to say. I tell them, *There is a plant that grows in ponds. Bogbean. Its stalk is thick as a thumb, its flowers white and furred as the ears of a dog, and at the top its buds are flushed pink with life. Pluck the plant from the water and thank the pond. One side of a bogbean leaf draws pus from a wound. The other side heals the cleansed flesh. Do you imagine, after all this, I'll tell you which side is which?*

I lift the noose from around my neck, step onto the

hard wood, feel the boards with my bare feet. Soon I will walk the deck of a ship and sail away.

Do not worry, Mother says to the crowd. *I will stay. I will tell you.*

In Mother's version of the story, the virgin sings and the afanc is so mesmerized, he crawls from the water and lays his head down in the virgin's lap to sleep, trustful as a child. When the villagers emerge to bind the afanc, the afanc's struggles crush the virgin. In the end, the afanc is taken to a new and better lake. The villagers have their village back. Only the virgin dies.

A witch is the daughter of a crone, a slut the daughter of a whore, and I am the drop that races along the threads until the whole bolt is ruined.

When they hang Mother, I am long gone. The air does not hold her up, though it embraces her all the same.

CASPER

The girls of the Unclaimed Baggage Depot—
Greenleaf, Alabama's, second-best and only other
unclaimed baggage store—found Casper in a
lime green suitcase. Like every Monday morning, the
owner had unloaded a truck filled with bags from cut-
rate airlines and a few bus terminals and left them in
the hot backroom for the girls to sort. That summer
Brittany had found, among other things, a pocket watch,
a left-handed bowling ball embossed with the name
Porkchop, and a ziplocked bag of used condoms. Valentina had found a Tiffany's letter opener, three tarot
decks, and a silver jar full of what they agreed were human remains. Amy Sue only halfheartedly participated.

She'd found, and pocketed, a pair of gold stud earrings, and had gotten a rash from a half-used bottle of hand lotion. Mostly, she watched Brittany and Valentina work while she texted her boyfriend, who was ignoring her lately, wishing that she worked at the Unclaimed Baggage SUPERSTORE™, the birthright of every thin, tan, popular teenage girl of Greenleaf, *her* destiny until she'd been caught shoplifting Red Bull and tampons from the local gas station. Girls who shoplifted did not work at the SUPERSTORE™. They sat in the backroom of the Depot, sweating, digging through a bag clearly owned by a pervert. Amy Sue threw yet another sparkly thong, missing half its sequins, into a trash bag.

The SUPERSTORE™ was the only reason anyone came to Greenleaf, and the Depot survived by dint of its rival's reflected glory. The SUPERSTORE™ was large and clean and popular. The Depot was messy and small, the last shop operating in a gray-stucco strip mall. The SUPERSTORE™ got the unclaimed bags from every major airline and drew people from miles away, the parking lot always full, the license plates from Mississippi, Texas, Florida. People came for the fantasy that they would snatch up what some careless rich person had left behind—a designer coat, an antique watch, a brand-new iPhone with *kisses, Chastity* engraved on the back. The SUPERSTORE™ played up the theater of it.

Every few hours, they let a customer open a bag in front of an audience.

Early in the summer, Valentina had tried to impress Amy Sue with the story of when she'd been selected. She'd been in middle school and it had been the most exciting day of her life. The girl working there had pulled Valentina's name out of the bowl in front of a whole crowd of people, given her the latex safety gloves, let her unzip the bag. The lotto winner got to choose one thing from the bag to keep, free, and Valentina still had the paperweight she'd found, a glass sphere the size of a baseball, with a shard at its heart. A chunk of the Berlin Wall? A moon rock? When she couldn't sleep, she held it in her hand until the glass was warm and she imagined that someday, when she needed it most, the heat of her body would crack it open and the shard inside would prove to be the key to a grand adventure.

"It's all fake," Amy Sue had told her. "They've already opened those bags. They take out anything really valuable and then plant mediocre shit."

What did Amy Sue know? She couldn't even get a job at the SUPERSTORE™. But, then, neither could Valentina. She wasn't pretty but she wasn't not pretty. She wasn't a cheerleader, but she wasn't in debate club or band, either, wasn't sure what her interests might turn out to be, except that she knew she wanted to be liked.

She had gone home that night and moved her paper-weight from her desk into her sock drawer.

Despite all this, Valentina still experienced a small thrill whenever she opened a new bag. As Amy Sue flicked a thong at Brittany, Valentina pulled a lime green suitcase off the pile and unzipped it. She began discarding the wads of crumpled newspaper from inside. Why didn't Amy Sue ever flick thongs at her? There was a lot of newspaper, and then, beneath it, an object almost as big as the suitcase. She pressed her palm against it. Solid. "Hey guys," Valentina said, and for a moment no one paid attention. Brittany was making a point of ignoring Amy Sue. Amy Sue was checking her phone. Valentina pulled the large object from the suitcase, surprised by how light it was. She set it upright on the concrete floor; it came to about her waist and was practically spherical, wrapped in colorful scarves like a festive mummy. She unwrapped one scarf, then another, the other girls finally noticed and drifted over to her, and the back room was suddenly quiet.

"What the fuck is that?" Brittany asked.

They all hoped for something different.

Brittany wanted it to be a discovery. Not a discovery to them, but something a museum would want. She imagined an object stolen from the halls of the British Museum, a grateful curator weeping at the object's safe return, promising to give Brittany anything she wanted, an internship, a tour of the back rooms. Someday, Brittany wanted to work for a museum, building dioramas and interactive exhibits, recording and sorting objects in a room that was cold and quiet and clean.

Valentina hoped it would be something she got credit for. Yes, any one of them could have opened the lime green bag, but it had been her and that counted for something.

Amy Sue hoped for something so spectacular that it would erase the summer up until this moment. She took so much shit from her friends at the SUPERSTORE™. But there was nothing under the scarves that could change that. "Maybe it's half a dude," she said. "Maybe his legs are in one of these other cases."

Valentina stopped unwinding.

"Don't be stupid," Brittany said, but her heart sped up.

"I'm serious," Amy Sue said, "last week, the Superstore girls opened this totally normal looking bag and they found a flare gun, five boxes of flares, porn mags, like old school, huge bushes, and a Big Bertha firecracker, the kind that blows your hands off."

Brittany wondered how a suitcase full of explosives got on a plane. Maybe the bags were confiscated at the airport? Maybe Amy Sue was full of shit.

"Wait a sec," Brittany said. She went into the employee

bathroom and put on the pair of yellow gloves they used to scrub the toilet. Valentina found herself pushed to the side and it was Brittany, not her, pulling away the scarves, one at a time, then removing more newspaper, peeling masking tape off bubble wrap, revealing, bit by bit, ears, white fur, a small and delicate face, pink glass eyes. The animal sat happily on his haunches, his fluffy belly protruding over his feet, peaceful, plump, pleased, even, with how things had turned out for him.

"What the fuck *is* that?" Amy Sue said, echoing Brittany, but softly, with reverence, because they already knew what it was. It was proof that they were meant to be in this back room at this exact moment. It was a reward for months and years of boredom and the size of the town where they lived and the distance of that town from any place they wanted to be. It was a taxidermied albino wallaby and it was the greatest thing to ever happen to the Depot, until it was the end of everything.

Caring for Casper that first week involved some false starts. Brittany forbade anyone from touching him without gloves because she'd read in *Smithsonian* magazine that this was what people did with truly valuable pieces. Once, Amy Sue strapped Casper into the passenger seat of Brittany's car as a joke, scaring Brittany half to death when she got in. Valentina, when no one was looking, did stroke the soft fur on his tummy because she knew she wasn't supposed to and it felt so nice. Brittany caught her once, *quit that*, she said, slapped Valentina's hand away, but Valentina *deserved* to touch him, because she had found Casper and she had thought of his name. After they'd named him, it was like he *wasn't* dead, he was their companion, the mascot of the Depot. At first, they kept him by the register, but customers kept trying to pet him and Amy Sue almost fought a guy who perched sunglasses on Casper's nose. *He's not a toy!* she yelled. They moved him near the door, on top of a stack of old typewriter cases, very cosmopolitan, until a customer bumped into him and knocked him off his perch. This was when Brittany realized that the safest place for Casper was in the window, the star of a display that she would create. Last semester, Brittany had built a ten-foot-tall model of the Eiffel Tower for the school's production of *Gigi* using chicken wire, a bucket of plaster, and sheets ripped into one-inch strips. She knew what she was doing. She cleaned out the space in the front floor-to-ceiling window, washed the window for the first time all summer, possibly for the first time in years. The Depot was so much brighter. Why hadn't she thought to do this at the beginning of the summer? She regretted the displays she'd missed: Fourth of July, maybe a beach theme. This would be the first of many homes she would build for Casper.

While Brittany made the display, Amy Sue and Valentina sat on the curb outside. They were not supposed to turn around until Brittany told them they could look. Amy Sue lit a cigarette and dangled it from her fingers. She rarely inhaled and she liked to see how long the ash could grow before it fell. All her friends smoked and she didn't like it much, but didn't want to be left behind.

Amy Sue got a text and laughed.

"What?" Valentina asked.

"Nothing," Amy Sue said. "People."

Valentina pulled her phone out, wishing she had a text message to be secretive about, and since she didn't, she bumped Amy Sue's arm, making the ash fall to the ground. "Sorry," Valentina said. She was happy to see that Amy Sue was freckling.

When Brittany came outside, Amy Sue said, "About time," and rolled her eyes, like, *god, who cares?* except she was excited too, they all were. They turned to face the display. "That's awesome," Valentina said, and Brittany didn't pay that much attention to her. She was focused on Amy Sue, who took her time, didn't speak right away, walked up close to the glass but didn't smudge it. As always, Valentina felt she'd made a mistake.

Towers built of cardboard boxes were draped in salmon tablecloths and there were tablecloths on the floor, too, dusted with sand. On the towers, where the edges of boxes jutted out, she'd put the small rubber animals lost by some child. On the ground were shells laid out in spirals, a rubber snake. In her mind, it was a desert, a wasteland. Casper she'd added last, off center to the left, so much larger than the child's toys that he was like a monster in the landscape, the pink of his eyes popping to match the background, his fur impossibly white.

"Casper looks happy," Amy Sue finally said, and she meant it. It was beautiful. "He looks like fucking Godzilla!"

Yes, Valentina thought. *That's what I should have said.*

That day, the Depot sold a broken pocket watch to a man who said he could use it for a costume. They sold a Discraft UltraStar regulation Frisbee. They sold a wooden falcon painted shiny black—an exact replica of the one from *The Maltese Falcon*—to a man who drove a motorcycle. He strapped the falcon to his back and revved out of the parking lot. They watched him disappear down the main street.

Three different people asked about Casper, and one man asked if he was for sale.

"No," Brittany said, though of course he was. The owner of the Depot wasn't there to contradict her. He was never there.

"Sorry," Amy Sue said to the customer, and gave the guy a big smile because she enjoyed being beautiful.

That night, Valentina made a box of mac and cheese. Her parents were out on their weekly date, dinner and a movie in the next town over. She always tried to enjoy having the house to herself—wasn't that what all teenagers wanted?—but the truth was she didn't like being alone at night. She ate the macaroni straight from the pot and played her music as loud as it went on her shitty little speaker. The house always seemed fragile when the windows were dark, the outside world pressing itself against the glass until she was afraid to stand too near, until she found herself paralyzed in the middle of the room. She imagined the glass exploding toward her. *It's because I have an amazing imagination*, she told herself.

She lay on the carpet in the middle of the room and thought about her paperweight. She would get up soon, as soon as she could, and take it out of her sock drawer, put it back where it belonged.

Brittany ate spaghetti with her parents. They both taught at the community college one town over and talked about a student they shared—a boy who had outbursts in class, but was, they thought, well-meaning. How much disruption until it was too much? They did not ask her about her day and she didn't tell them about the display; they would have asked too many questions and made too many suggestions. She felt trampled by their helpfulness. She hated that during the summer she couldn't go to her room and pretend to do homework.

Instead, they watched television together, a documentary called *Blackfish* about Tilikum, an Orca whale in captivity who had killed three different people. The whales were so sad, seen from above, trapped in what was basically a bathtub for them. *That whale just wants to escape*, Brittany thought, and found herself tearing up and looking down at her phone to distract herself, flipping through snapchats until her mother told her to knock it off. A whale looked at the camera through thick glass and Brittany thought of Casper behind the windows in the display, sitting in the dark on the tablecloth, his pink glass eyes glinting when the rare car passed. Tomorrow she would build him a little nest, the way she would have when she was a kid and she still tucked her stuffed animals in, still left snacks out for them, in case they came alive while she was gone and woke up hungry.

Amy Sue went to the most cliché of parties: a friend's parents were out of town. It was fine, nothing special and nothing bad either and she was a little tipsy and told some girls who worked at the SUPERSTORE™ about the Depot's new window display, about Casper. "We're coming for you," she joked, except she wasn't, and she couldn't quite understand why she wanted to brag about the shitty place until she realized she was actually bragging about Brittany. Brittany was kind of amazing, an artist, and Amy Sue was tipsy enough that she wished Brittany were there, was tempted to text her, but didn't.

The music was loud, Amy Sue was getting another drink while some guy threw up in the sink, when a girl came into the kitchen. She was breathless with excitement. She told Amy Sue that another girl had just walked in on Rayna fucking Amy Sue's boyfriend in the upstairs bathroom. The red Solo cup of beer fell out of her hand. *Well, that explains why he's been ignoring me*, she thought. Her flats were now wet. She liked those flats. She walked out into the living room, and saw Rayna coming down the stairs, and all Amy Sue could think was that Rayna already worked for the SUPERSTORE™. She didn't need anything else. Rayna walked up to her, was about to speak, and Amy Sue did the one thing she could think to do. She punched Rayna in the face. Someone shrieked and the room spun a little as Amy Sue spun too, walked back out of the room, and, in the time-honored tradition of parties going wrong, locked herself in the bathroom to cry.

It could have ended there but it didn't. Her friends talked to her through the door. Her boyfriend arrived. She screamed at him. She took his phone and scrolled through his pictures and there they were, naked pictures of that bitch. She texted them to herself, dropped her boyfriend's phone in the toilet, and then sent the pictures to a dozen different people. The rest of the night was a blur, she drank more, and though she insisted afterward that the slut deserved it, she woke up hungover and ashamed. She turned the shower on to try to cover the sounds of her heaving from her parents. She wished she'd punched her boyfriend instead, sent the world a picture of his dick, which he'd texted to her so many times, thinkng of u, wher u at?, or only the image, the shaft a little bent to the left, no caption, its hardness doing all the talking.

She splashed her face with cold water, and stared at herself. She looked the same. She rinsed out her mouth, spit, then brushed her hair up into the high, tight ponytail that meant business.

The next morning, the sky was blue and a brief rain had cleared out the humidity, a small, short-lived miracle. Brittany arrived at the Depot first, as she always did; she was proud to be the one the owner trusted with the keys. It was a big responsibility. She was listening to the radio, singing along, Tilikum out of her mind, happy enough that she didn't see what had happened until she got out of her car.

The window of the Depot was smashed in, shattered glass all across the sidewalk. The display was demolished, and not only from the rock lying inside but from hands that had riffled through it. The cardboard boxes were cracked open like skulls. The shells broken underfoot, mixed up with the glass and the pieces of the little animals, everything destroyed. Everything except for Casper. She didn't need to go inside to know he was gone. If he wasn't in the window, he'd been taken, and she couldn't bring herself to go inside anyway. The violence of the scene frightened her; if she went in alone, somehow she would be the one blamed, she would be broken on the floor next to the objects she'd let be destroyed. So she stood where she was on the sidewalk, wondering why, *why*, because who would bother to attack something so totally unimportant to anyone but her.

Amy Sue and Valentina arrived together twenty minutes later.

"Jesus shit," Amy Sue said. *Fuck fuck fuck*, she thought, as if thinking that word over and over would keep her from thinking anything else.

Valentina stared. Her heart was racing, the way people said it should during moments like this. She was excited. This was exciting. Horrible, yes, but like a movie. She looked at Amy Sue and Brittany and didn't say anything.

There were wet spots on the tablecloths. The girls leaned as close as they could to the display. It smelled of liquor and piss.

"They took Casper," Brittany finally said.

I knew this was going to happen, Brittany thought, even though that was crazy. I should have gone back for him last night.

Fuck fuck fuck, Amy Sue sang to herself. Fuck fuck fuck.

Fucking cool. Valentina smiled.

They called the cops, who took some photos. They called the owner, who said he'd have someone out as soon as he could to replace the window. He'd be by later. They swept up the glass. They folded the cardboard boxes flat. They tied up the debris in the tablecloths and hauled the salmon-pink bundles to the dumpster. Amy Sue reluctantly told them about the party, the fight, but not about the naked pictures she'd sent. "I know they did this, all the girls who work at the Superstore," she said. "To get back at me."

Valentina had gotten the naked pictures of Rayna on her phone from a friend in the small hours of the morning, but she didn't say anything. Someone along the chain had made it into a gif, with *fat slut* written at the bottom and little tacos dancing in the background. Valentina had sent a boyfriend naked pictures of herself many times, *didn't everyone?* and while she had always been intimidated by Amy Sue, a little in awe of her, now she was afraid of her and knew, finally, that she was better than Amy Sue.

"Those fucking bitches," Amy Sue muttered as they

swept up broken glass, careful not to get the small shards lodged in the thin rubber of her flip flops. It was her hangover that was making her feel so sick. She was sweating beer.

By noon, they'd cleaned the mess and taped some of the broken-down cardboard across the window with duct tape. They wrote OPEN on it in black Sharpie. The Depot, which had always looked ramshackle, now looked positively sinister. They went inside, turned on the overhead fluorescent light, and sat on the floor side by side, backs propped against a shelf of books. No one came in.

"We have to do something," Amy Sue said. "My step-dad has cans of spray paint in the garage. We can write Bitch Sluts across the windows of the Superstore. Everyone will see that. Write Fuck You! in red letters."

"That's fucking stupid," Brittany said. "What matters is Casper."

Valentina nodded. "We should egg the place instead." She hated bad smells more than anything else.

Brittany ignored her. "I'm not writing dumb shit on the wall. We need to get inside." She turned to Amy Sue. "You're there with them all the time. You know how."

"If we're inside we can throw eggs on the wedding dresses," Valentina said. If there was going to be an adventure, Valentina wanted to come. And she'd always wanted to see the back rooms, the secret places. She'd loved her paperweight, but she was older now. There had to be so much more.

Brittany was going to save Casper and she wasn't going to bring him back to the Depot, either. Casper wasn't going to be trapped anymore. She wouldn't tell the other girls her plans and she couldn't give a shit what Amy Sue and her friends fought about. She was sure this was Amy Sue's fault. Fucking Amy Sue who already had everything she wanted and had now fucked this up for Brittany and just as Brittany was starting to feel like they could be friends.

And Amy Sue, she had to retaliate. She had to retaliate because otherwise the other popular girls would know she hadn't, and that would be admitting that what had happened to the Depot was not only because of her but her fault entirely, because she'd been drunk and angry, because it was easier to hurt another girl than admit she was hurt herself. It would be admitting that she didn't *deserve* to retaliate. She pushed the thought from her mind. Rayna had fucked her boyfriend. She'd hold on to that.

"Back of the Superstore. Midnight," Amy Sue said.

Valentina nodded. God this was great.

Brittany found a sliver of glass in the pad of her hand

and pulled it out slowly, surprised by how much it stung and how little it bled. "We're going in and out. Nothing stupid," she said, and Amy Sue and Valentina nodded.

The SUPERSTORE™ looked different in the dark. Both less impressive—it was just a glorified warehouse, after all—and more untouchable. Amy Sue was there first. She pulled her phone out of her back pocket to check the time—five to midnight—decided she wouldn't look at it again. Too bright. The cicadas were so loud she felt like she was drowning in them.

The plan was simple. She knew the employee code for the back door. Get in, get to the employee lounge, find something of theirs to fuck up no matter what Brittany said, find Casper, leave, quick as anything. She'd even brought the pair of yellow toilet cleaning gloves. No finger prints, she'd say to Valentina and Brittany, except they still weren't there. Maybe they weren't coming. Maybe they'd decided this was Amy Sue's problem.

Next to the door was a wedge of concrete the SUPER-STORE™ girls used to prop the door when they stood out back having a smoke. If Valentina and Brittany came, they could meet her inside. She punched in the code, set down the chunk of concrete, and snuck inside.

———

Valentina was still at home. What did people wear to a break in? She put on jeans and a black hoodie, but that was boring. She changed into a short dress. Like a James Bond girl, except those girls usually ended up dead, didn't they?

What had they done to Casper? Brittany was at home, waiting, picturing poor Casper sliced open, his guts spewing fluff. What was even inside a taxidermied animal? She'd never checked. If they cut him, would his skin peel back over the mold, sagging, relieved to give up pretending to be alive?

She slipped on her flip flops and sat on the edge of the bed.

Her parents finally turned their light out. She was already late. She tiptoed, as quiet as she could be, though she knew that even if they heard a soft noise, they would never think it was her.

The employee lounge was the first door on the right. No windows, no one can see, Amy Sue told herself, though she felt panicky. Turning on the light was fine. The walls were bare except for a motivational poster that said, *Dreams. Not Just for Sleeping!* An eagle soared above a mountain. Rayna's employee cubby was empty. Well, that was fine. This was about more than Rayna now anyway. It hadn't been just Rayna she'd told about the window display. It was all of them.

Valentina arrived twenty minutes late, wearing black leggings and a tight black tank top. She was a freaking tomb raider tonight. She didn't care that Amy Sue would laugh—she felt like a ninja, an explorer, and an assassin. Better than Amy Sue. She wasn't a bitch like that. When she snuck through the propped door and into the hall, she saw the light under a closed door and tiptoed past. She didn't care what the other girls were doing.

The main room of the SUPERSTORE™ was enormous in the dark, the racks of clothes endless, but this wasn't what Valentina had come for. This part of the store she could see any day. She walked down the main aisle, past Women's Wear, Swimsuits, Men's Shoes, a hat display that looked like bouquets of exotic flowers in the dim light. Past the electronics counter, past the Happily Ever After grotto of lost wedding dresses (she'd left the eggs at home). Finally, she found the side door she remembered from middle school. It was the door through which they'd carried her unopened bag, the paperweight undiscovered inside. This was the place. She turned the knob and, though she didn't expect it, the door opened.

Brittany got to the SUPERSTORE™ forty minutes late and wasn't surprised to find the door propped; Amy Sue wasn't the kind of person who waited. Brittany slipped inside, saw the light under the first door, and opened it to find Amy Sue writing on a card table in ketchup.

"They only have ketchup packets so this is taking forever," Amy Sue said, motioning to the squeezed-out rectangles that littered the floor. Her yellow gloves were red. The letters on the table spelled S L U

"Have you seen Casper?"

"Not in here. Or Valentina either. I guess she got cold feet."

Brittany looked around the little room, as if Casper could be there without Amy Sue having noticed. She hadn't thought past this, had assumed Casper would be there, and she'd grab him and go.

"You mean you haven't looked anywhere else?"

The truth was, Amy Sue had kind of forgotten about Casper.

"I'm sure he'll turn up," Amy Sue said.

This wasn't what they were supposed to be doing. The SUPERSTORE™ was huge. Brittany would never find Casper on her own; Amy Sue knew the place better than she did. There was a little television mounted up on a wall. Brittany walked to it, unplugged it, lifted it—it was lighter than Casper, tiny really—and threw it on the floor. The screen shattered, the cheap plastic exterior cracked.

"Fuck," Amy Sue said, her work on the card table made suddenly cheap and violent all at once.

Brittany looked down at the television, disappointed. No sparks, no explosion. "There," she said. "We've fucked their shit up. Now are you going to help? Or are you going to keep being pathetic? Because this," she gestured at the table, "is fucking pathetic."

Amy Sue straightened up, held her gory hands in front of her.

Through the door, down the stairs, Valentina was in the basement of the SUPERSTORE™.

The ceiling was low and there were racks upon racks of unopened bags, stacked on top of each other, all colors and patterns. She had her cell phone flashlight on and she wished that someone else was with her so that she could say *wow* and *this is so cool!*

Valentina had never been well liked. Maybe in elementary school, but middle school, and then high school—she'd faded into the background. She feared she was closest to the girls at the Depot and the girls at the Depot didn't like her much. They knew she was lacking something. Brittany was always fiddling with a project, organizing shelves, and then asking her opinion and Valentina never knew what to say. *I think it needs more drama*, she might offer, and Brittany would nod as if to say, obviously, but what drama? What? And Valentina had nothing more to add. And Amy Sue. Amy Sue, who wore the promise of a better life in her slender limbs and her confidence.

But who could lack in the face of all of this? Valentina dragged her fingertips over the luggage. Her hands felt naked, daring, no latex gloves this time. Finally, she chose a blue suitcase, chose it because it seemed the most ordinary a suitcase could be; wasn't that the way to find treasure, wasn't the most precious thing always inside the most boring exterior? It was heavy as she lifted it and set it on the floor. As she unzipped it, her fingers shook.

The top layer was clothes. Soft, that made sense, to protect what might be underneath. The layer below, clothes too. The bra of a woman with much larger breasts than Valentina's. She dumped the clothes in a pile beside her. Beneath the clothes, toiletries. Two pairs of ladies' heels. Two ten-pound hand weights. That was the reason the bag had been so heavy. The weights were the least romantic thing Valentina could imagine.

She took down another suitcase. Fancy looking this time. Fleur-de-lis or some shit on the outside. Opened it, the top layer clothes, clothes, more fucking clothes, men's clothes this time, and a Dopp kit with a small bottle of shaving lotion, nothing, nothing good, and she opened another suitcase and another, and she did find a few odd things—a bag of wheat pennies, a hair dryer broken down into ten different pieces, a dildo like a fucking horse cock and she put that in her purse because she didn't know what else to do. Her phone's flashlight cut across the debris, casting sharp shadows. There was nothing here. Her paperweight—it had been a lie. Not a medium thing, planted to represent something better, but a better thing, a best thing, because the truth was people were boring. They were predictable. When they traveled, they packed underwear and toothpaste and sneakers that smelled and then the whole suitcase smelled and no one seemed to care that they were ruining the little they had.

Valentina stood, stepped across the clothes until she was free of her own mess. At the end of the row of suitcases was a cage with a latch. She lifted it, heard its hard metal clang, cast her light across the shelves of confiscated items. A few knives that would be sanitized and moved to a locked glass case upstairs. That flare gun, the one Amy Sue had talked about. The girls would like to see that. She opened a box of flares, shoved one in the gun, stuck the gun in the back of her leggings, *assassin!* and that was when she saw him, sitting on the floor. Casper. Too white in the dark, truly like a ghost. She went to him, held out her hands, paused because she wasn't wearing gloves and what would Brittany say, then lifted him to herself and hugged him as tight as she could.

"I did it," she whispered.

She held Casper close and walked out of the basement, leaving an explosion of objects behind her.

"You think this is pathetic?" Amy Sue was yelling. It was pathetic. She knew that. *Fuck fuck fuck*. But she couldn't admit that, especially to Brittany. "What is more pathetic than you making a window display for a place no one is ever going to visit? The Depot is a shit-hole. This town is a shithole."

"I'm going to find Casper," Brittany said, strangely calm now that she'd destroyed the television. "I don't need your help."

Valentina listened outside, heard them yelling, and smiled. "Hey!" she said, walking in. She was too loud. Both girls shrieked and jumped and Amy Sue pressed a ketchup covered hand to her heart, smearing her shirt and bare skin.

"Casper!" Brittany cried, and pulled him from Valentina's arms.

"Fucking girl ninja here," Amy Sue said, taking in Valentina's outfit, happy to have someone other than Brittany to fight with, someone so easy to pick on. "Where the hell have you been?" Brittany was caressing Casper. "You're like *so* late," Amy Sue said, and all she could think was, *I couldn't even find Casper.* Valentina, fucking *Valentina*, found him. She turned and swiped across the letters on the table with her gloved hand. Ketchup sprayed across the floor like blood and Brittany turned her back to shield Casper, then walked with him to the far corner of the room and set him down, knelt in front of him, smoothed his fur with the back of her hands, as if they were safer than her fingers, less dirty, less aggressive, as if she were trying to save Casper from the room, from Amy Sue's contaminating influence.

Amy Sue watched Brittany caress Casper and felt close to tears. She wanted Brittany to touch her face. Did she? God. She wanted to be anywhere but here. She dropped her gloves to the floor in two wet slaps.

Valentina watched them. No one had thanked her. Brittany stood and walked to Amy Sue and asked, "Are you finished?"

Amy Sue responded, "Whatever." No one was paying any attention to Valentina. Like she didn't matter, wasn't there, exactly like it had been the entire summer, except now she knew that Amy Sue was a bad person, and Brittany, well, Brittany was as wrong as she had been, enthralled by Amy Sue, thinking there was something there when there wasn't. Both of them treated her like garbage. She felt like the glass of all the windows in the world were exploding toward her and the glass didn't even cut her because she was a ghost like Casper.

Her hand shook. She pulled the flare gun from the band of her leggings, took aim, and fired.

Casper burst into flames.

Amy Sue would never go back to the Depot. As Casper went up, she reached both arms out, her legs frozen, her mouth open but no sound coming out. *I'm in love with Brittany*, she thought. *Brittany will never forgive me for this*.

Later, Amy Sue would date women and men, move to Atlanta, do fine for herself, and sometimes, rarely, think of Brittany and smile, then think of Rayna, who had never forgiven her, and feel ashamed. Then she would push the memory from her mind.

Brittany would have expected to scream or weep. This was worse than her demolished window display, worse than being told she was a bad kisser. Worse than the time she'd found her father crying after her mother had slapped him. Instead, her eyes were so dry they burned with Casper. Perhaps that was the chemicals in the air. Perhaps she had discovered a talent for giving up what was already gone.

Years later, designing the set for a play in Nashville, she would walk down the street and see a taxidermied albino squirrel in the window of an antiques shop. She would touch the glass, look at the squirrel trapped behind it, and remember Casper going out in that blaze of glory, like a Viking funeral. Casper, that fluffy sweet goofball, a warrior on his way to Valhalla, and she wouldn't believe it, but she was crying and it was because she was happy, a sweet memory when she had expected to feel sad.

None of them knew how long it took for Casper to burn himself out. The skin went up like newspaper, the glue beneath it flamed blue, his attentive ears gone in puffs of smoke, the wire cage that had held the skin taught folding in on itself as Casper made a final bow. He died for the last time.

Amy Sue and Brittany did not speak as they left the scene. Casper's sticky ketchup blood was splattered across the floor as if he had exploded, tiny droplets in a spray pattern. Only Valentina remained. She had never seen anything so beautiful. The shot itself had been almost quiet, a small pop, but the noise of the impact was like one man punching another. This would be one of the greatest moments of her life, not because she was proud of it, because she wasn't, not exactly, but then, it was so rare to hold a moment in your hand, to be the one to make a finite amount of time last forever.

AN APOLOGY OF
SORTS TO JUNE

If you believe nothing else, believe that I never meant to run over our cat. There were other things I did, things I'm not proud of, but what marriage ever ended smoothly? I'll say upfront, in the spirit of total honesty, I shouldn't have written "bitch" in poison on the front lawn of your new boyfriend's house. I know you know it was me, and in my defense, his lawn was asking for it. How much time does he spend on his knees, trimming away the imperfections with his sewing scissors? When does he have time to fuck you, with a lawn like a golf course?

But that isn't the point. The point is that a car is a big object and Jelly was stupid. Animals should distrust cars, the smell of death on them—exhaust, leather, pine air freshener—but not Jelly. Jelly shed fur in clumps, peed in corners, was old, slightly blind, and mostly deaf. She was a loved cat. Our daughter loved that cat. It didn't make Jelly a good cat. Jelly was a terrible cat. Our daughter loves me, and you wouldn't say that made me a good husband.

I ran over Jelly as I was backing out of the garage, a small thump, like running over a forgotten bag of groceries. When I got out to look, there was Jelly by the left back tire, on her side, ribs popped in like a broken umbrella. I have never liked that cat. If you were honest, you'd admit you never liked her either. But at that moment, I'd never wanted two seconds back so badly. A nothing bit of time, the flare of a match, a sip of coffee, a handshake that spreads the flu. Give me those few seconds back, I thought, and I'll give you every second this year that I spent respectfully enjoying the delightful sight of a woman's breasts. No, I won't apologize. You used to think I was funny. Does the dickhead with the lawn make you smile at deep fried Snickers or tap dancing, plumcots or the Wisconsin Dells? Never laughing at the people who love those things, never cruel, but at the fact of their existence, the why of them, in that there is no why, which is the essence of delight. Because I did that for you.

I'm getting to the baseball bat. That bat was an act of

mercy but you don't want to see it that way. The animal was suffering. I *wanted* to call 911 but it was a cat, the kind of situation that calls for an adult to take care of it and I was that adult, whether I wanted to be or not. Whether I was capable or not. Who hasn't been forced to be an adult, to live up to that incredible lie?

I got a towel out of the trunk and wrapped it around her body, a little nest, but Jelly wouldn't stop screaming, short high-pitched yowls. I sat next to her, tried to pet her. It seemed kind, better to die with someone's hand on you. Cats are very small. You don't think about it. Under that fur, they're barely there, a bundle of twigs. I kept my hand on her head, moving it slowly until I was at the nape. I could simply crush it, snap it quickly. My hand hovered, ready, and that's when Jelly bit the flesh between my thumb and forefinger. You will be glad to know, it hurt. It hurt like a bitch.

The kind thing—that's all I was trying to do. The kind thing, for that stupid fucking cat that our daughter loves. I can do the kind thing when it's hard. The kind thing when it's easy, well, you know I've always preferred big gestures. I went into the garage, looking for the kind thing. The tool case; a tub of recycling; boxes of clothes for the Salvation Army that have sat for years, helping no one. I picked up the baseball bat.

I swear, Jelly was the stupidest cat who ever lived, but

when I came back out and she looked at me with her flat cat eyes, we understood each other. I had the bat over my head. Where to hit her? What would be fastest and cleanest? I wanted to do it. I saw myself doing it and the memory of that imagining feels almost the same as the memory of action. It would have been the kind thing to do, and I might have done it. I want to believe I was going to do it. That was when you drove up, our daughter June in the back seat of the van, her small face pressed against the tinted window.

"Stay in the car, sweetie," you said.

I dropped the bat, the aluminum clattering against the concrete like breaking glass.

You didn't speak. You bent down to Jelly and in one fluid motion scooped her up. Jelly bit you too, but you didn't drop her. You cradled her to your chest, enveloping her in the towel, holding her firmly but lightly, like a crying child, a half-formed thought. *Hush*, you murmured. *Hush now. I've got you.*

You told me to get our daughter out of the car, to take her inside and watch her while you drove Jelly to the vet. You said to try to do this one small thing. You looked ashamed of me. But I don't think you had it right. Sometimes it's better to stop the pain quickly, not drag it out, not if the ending will be the same either way.

MARY READ IS A CROSSDRESSING PIRATE, THE RAGING SEAS, 1720

It is easier to be a man. My mother teaches me this when I am small, though that isn't how she says it. She pulls my arms through my dead brother's coat, looks at my newly cropped hair, crosses herself at the resemblance, a sin to bring his body back to life. *Stand straight,* she tells me, *and if you must speak, pretend shyness.* I have never been shy a day in my life, of course, but I already relish playing at a role. I hug my grandmother and she touches my head, promises my mother the money owed a son, and asks us not to return. I thank her for the lesson, well-learned, that if the world will give money to a dead boy and not a live girl, then I will stay a daughter inside a son, a sister inside a brother, the man my sheath, the woman my blade.

———

I enlist in the British army. *What a thrill to be a man!* I say, in the arms of my lover. We both look splendid in our uniforms.

But all this violence, he says, and rolls atop me, pins me to the mattress for another round.

He dies in the way soldiers do, suddenly and young.

I sail the seas and am impressed into service on a pirate ship, sail beside Anne Bonny and Calico Jack on the good ship *Revenge* and no one knows me for a woman. I kill men in duels. I stand in the crow's nest at night and look at the stars and when my shift ends, I retreat to bed, to my Annie. She is also a cross dressing pirate. I love to woo the woman in her.

Come, my love, and surrender to me. You are Patience herself, waiting for me this long day, trapped in my cabin. My captive Princess, my darling.

Annie flips me onto my back for another round of lovemaking, but I keep on rolling, until I am on top again.

When we finish, I tell her the sea is so calm tonight, the moon so bright, I can see a pod of whales, their wet humps flashing silver. *Imagine us,* I say, *home in bonny England, sucking our husband's syphilitic cocks, waiting for the soup to boil.* Annie laughs between my breasts. We only wield a needle to mend a sail or stitch a wound. We eat the soup the cook makes. We have been on this voyage long enough that the cured meat is gone, the soup a thin disguise for old potatoes.

Imagine, she sighs, wistful, and I think of the red currants I found in a hedgerow while I was a soldier, how they tasted fresh off the stem, warm from the sun. How I picked too many, gathered a mound in a kerchief to bring to my soldier-love. By the time I gifted them, they were more stain than berry.

When we are captured, it is quicker to be a man. The crew are swiftly hanged. Annie and I plead our bellies, for it is true, we grow lush with our pirate children, children destined to be wild and untamable like the mothers who fucked them into life and strong and steady like the mothers who will bear them.

I do not know how Annie dies. As for me, it's a bloody, violent death, and I fight bravely to the last. Yet when the coroner notes the cause of death, he writes childbirth, instead of the truth, that I died in battle against a daughter even stronger than myself, impatient to be free.

THE DISNEYLAND
OF MEXICO

I.

In the cab, squeezed between your host mother and sister, no seatbelts, your mouth open like a fish waiting for a hook: this is the moment you realize that you don't speak Spanish. You were prepared to speak it awkwardly, prepared to feel a little foolish, but you weren't prepared for this. These women speak a different language than your high school Spanish teacher, whose Midwestern accent forms each word like a pebble, distinct and hard. *Libro. Bolígrafo. Yo soy. Tú eres.* These two women speak a language that doesn't have pauses. It is fast and slick and impossible to hold.

Hola. Me llamo Amy, you said to them when they picked you up from the exchange program's office in

Pachuca; not an office really, a second story apartment with a pink toilet, mismatched furniture, and green walls that seemed to absorb rather than reflect light. *What am I doing here?* you asked yourself and all the answers: *improving my Spanish, getting into a good college, going on my first adventure*, were inadequate in the face of the rust on the pink toilet.

But your host family can't say Amy. They say *Amí*, as if you are loved this far away from home. Gabi, your new mother, and María, your new sister, take you to the cab where you learn that you don't speak Spanish, have never spoken Spanish, will probably never speak Spanish, will die alone at the age of sixteen in Pachuca, Mexico, having misunderstood the word *stop* for *go*, and crossing the street you will be crushed by one of the buses that career past the cramped yellow cab in the fading evening light.

These are the things that happen to you that first week, before you can parse sound into sentences:

You move into your room. It's at the back of the three-bedroom apartment, small, with a closet that does not close and a window that looks over a neighbor's back patio, twin bed against the wall, with a pale blue comforter and an old teddy bear that you keep under your arm at night. Because you are a teenager, because you are terrified and lonely, this room becomes a sanctuary. You put two photographs on the nightstand: one of your little brother, mother, and father, and one of your best friends, three girls smiling in winter coats.

You discover that you are afraid of the shower; it's electric. You hadn't believed it at first. *Eléctrico.* Surely it meant something else? Then you saw the box on the wall, below the nozzle. It hums, like a swarm of bees. You imagine being electrocuted, the water on your skin evaporating in a sizzling series of stings, and you stay as far away from the box as you can.

María is nineteen and she and her friends are already at the *universidad.* Her friends are all boys and you can't remember a single name. They don't speak English either and you don't say a word. You smile and nod or smile and shake your head. You have never smiled this much. The muscles in your face hurt.

You figure out how to use your calling card to call home. You think that talking to your parents will make you feel better but it makes you feel worse. In Minneapolis, July is hot and humid and mosquitos feast on thick white calves. The Mississippi churns brown, the parks around the lakes are green, and people rent canoes and sunburn as they paddle the Lake of the Isles. When you call home, your parents tell you that your brother's up in the Boundary Waters with his Boy Scout troop and they are taking a salsa class together. They sound unexpectedly gleeful that you are both out of the house. When they ask how it's going, you tell the truest lie and say you're learning a lot.

You don't tell them that Pachuca is starting to make you superstitious. Just small things: a song you know on the radio, a billboard for a movie you've seen, a moment of silence in your room when you can't hear anything at all, not even the traffic from the street, not even the sound of Gabi humming tunelessly while she boils beans in a large black pot. They comfort you, these signs that don't mean anything; it is as if you are being watched over.

You eat a sheep brain taco. María nearly dies laughing as you spit the crumbly brown filling into your hand.

Your host mother Gabi destroys all your underwear. Once she discovers the stains of many, many past periods, she takes you to the roof of the apartment where an old washer sits under an awning. There she washes them, hangs them on a line in the sun, finds they still have dark brown spots, and puts you in rubber gloves. She takes out what you eventually realize is bleach and proceeds to make you scrub it into the crotch of every pair. Then you put them back in the washing machine.

When they come out every single one is a rag; the bleach has eaten through the cotton. At a *supermercado* as big as a Costco, you buy a twelve pack of new underwear that doesn't fit quite right. It itches and the elastic digs into your inner thighs. You use your old underwear to dust the ceramic angels.

Ceramic angels: Gabi owns about twenty ceramic angels. Every morning you eat a baloney sandwich in your pajamas, then you do chores that Gabi has pantomimed for you. You beat the couch cushions (Gabi lifts one, hits it, hands it to you, you put it back on the couch, she shakes her head, picks up the same cushion, hits it, you hit it, you hit it again for good measure, and she smiles, and you set it down). Because you beat them every day, there is no satisfying puff of dust. If Gabi isn't in the room, you don't even bother picking them up, you just smack them with your palm so she hears it. The ceramic angels require more time. Every little figurine, every fat baby and tall, elegant Gabriel has to be taken off, dusted, the shelf wiped, and then put back in its exact spot. Your acceptance of these chores surprises you, not because you've been a rebellious teenager but because you've never, until now, considered rebelling and you've discovered you won't. You are like a dog, answering to a few understood commands, then waiting, ears pricked, to see what happens next.

And that is the essence of it. Sight. The wind, fierce and cold even in the summer, pushing the husk of a tamale down an empty cobblestone street on a Sunday evening; a woman who sits on the curb every day, her purple *serape* wrapped around her knees, selling hot, sugary *churros*; the lithe ceramic angel with blue eyes, so light it seems to be leaping, with a wing that has been glued back on. The superglue makes a scar down its back. It is your favorite angel.

Then, to your surprise, in your second week, clumps of sound turn into phrases, some of which are familiar. Verbs reenter your vocabulary and conversations are no longer things that happen *to* you. No longer do you say simply, *Yes* or *Tired* or *What?* Now you say, *It is nice today, I am hungry, I walked to the park, Please, repeat that more slowly.*

II.

You don't understand what *fiesta de la espuma* is until you are on the dance floor and the ceiling opens up, dumping soap suds all over the thin blue top and short black skirt that María lent you because your jeans and Ramones T-shirt were *grosera* and *bien fea*. Good ugly. But good ugly means very ugly. You are *bien gringa*, *very* gringa, and she has taken you under her wing.

When you arrive at the disco, she takes you into the bathroom and lays out her makeup on the counter: the black eyeliner, mascara, blue eye shadow, and red lipstick that Gabi doesn't want her wearing because it makes her look like a *princesa de la noche*. Gabi, María tells you, doesn't trust her, but you can't tell if that's true or if Gabi simply doesn't trust men, or both. You wonder sometimes where María's father is, if that is why she and Gabi fight sometimes. Their fights are sudden, loud, and then over as quickly. Not at all like your family, where fights are rare but linger.

María does herself first, layering black pencil until she has Cleopatra eyes, then she turns you to her and tickles your eyelashes, scrapes across your eyelids, smacks your hand away when you reach up to scratch your face, not thinking. When you look back at the mirror, you don't look like yourself. You are a raccoon with blood-stained lips. María pronounces that you look *bien chida* and you take her word for it. You want to look good tonight, like you are the same age as María, and just as confident.

Near the dance floor, you find the table where María's

boys are lounging, each sitting low and casual in their seats. You know them all now: Ramón, with glasses, Jorge, with bad acne scarring his left cheek, Luis, who is quiet and painfully thin, Anselmo, the tallest, and Manuel, who is twenty, with light brown eyes and a gray front tooth. Manny works at a *panadería*, a bakery that sells baguettes, rolls, sugar-crusted twists and horseshoes, churros, and cakes, frosted, tall, with heavy, syrup-soaked peaches on top. When you met him he sold Gabi a bag of rolls and he too pronounced your name *Amí*. Of course, you didn't understand what he was saying but his voice was warm and a little quiet, intimate. Leaving the bakery, you wanted to go right back and see him again.

Now you are Manny crazy. You've decided you want to kiss him, though you don't know how to go about accomplishing that, as you've never been kissed. The three girls in the picture on your dresser have already been kissed, even Heather, who you were sure would go to college pure as the snow, came back from a cruise to Alaska with a picture of a boy named George and a story about a swimming pool. You are the last one—and sometimes, as you lie on your bed in Pachuca, thinking about Manny and the smell of bread, you feel like you're the last one in the world.

You're at a disadvantage, you tell yourself, because

you came to the boy crazy phase late. That sudden awareness of boy's legs and hands arrived at the same time as your new breasts, which in the last year have changed from small, soft rises with puffy bee sting nipples into enough to almost fill out a B cup. You waited so long that you stopped expecting them, didn't notice them until your mother said you were "popping out" of your bra and made you try on one of hers. In the bathroom, changing into your mother's worn-out black bra, you studied yourself over the sink. There was enough there to create a slight shadow from the overhead light. When you pressed them with your hands, they gave like breasts. There was no other way to describe that strange, soft flesh.

You haven't found the right word for your chest yet. In your mind you've tested out options: tits, boobs, rack, fun bags, *tetas*. Spanish is no help, the language impossibly sexual, even when it isn't on the tongues of men catcalling you on the street. *Amor. Ángel.* You respect the men who are honest, who come out and say it. *Que tetas, mamí, gringa.* Tonight, in María's blue top, your chest looks deflated in the draped cotton.

Dancing hasn't started yet but the music is so loud it slaps your ears. It isn't just noise; it's nearly pain, like the air on a winter day when it's beyond cold. Manny sits between Luis and Anselmo, and you sit beside

Ramón and watch Manny. Even though no one can hear you, you say *hola* and resist the urge to cover your ears.

The boys nod and smile at you, sip *cervezas*, and María and Anselmo hold hands under the table as if no one notices. You are the only one who doesn't drink. At first, the boys teased you for not drinking, called you *niña* and then tried to make you say curse words. *Pendejo. Chinga tu madre. Puta.* You refused to repeat them, but you learned. They don't expect you to drink anymore and you use *pendejo* as a greeting, like they do. *Hola pendejo.* Everyone laughs. Hey asshole, hey.

María and Anselmo are the first to get up and dance. The dance floor is still only half full, so you can watch them without distraction. They press close on the dance floor and you can't help but stare at her red dress hiking up over his pant leg, their bodies dipping and rising in sync. Then the floor is jammed with bodies, you lose sight of María, and the other boys insist that you go out there too. They dance with you in a circle, like you've danced with your girlfriends at high school homecoming. They all smile. They are incredibly friendly. Manny smiles too. His smile looks the same as those around him, though you try to read into it something more. Soon they all find girls to dance with—a girl with black hair to her waist takes Manny and pulls him away—and you sit back down, too embarrassed to dance up to a stranger and too embarrassed to dance alone.

It's Ramón who eventually notices that you are by yourself and he comes over to sit with you. He says something. You shake your head and touch your ear. *It's too loud.* Speaking in signs comes so naturally to you now that you almost prefer this inability to use words.

He stands and offers you his hand, which you try to refuse, but he doesn't let you. On the dance floor, he stands in front of you, then his leg is between yours, his hands are on your hips. You try to move with him, convinced it should come naturally to you, but you stumble and he has to catch you. Your thighs sweat in María's faux-leather skirt.

Ramón smiles and taps your arm as if to say, *it's fine. No te preocupes.* Then he pulls you toward him again, but he keeps his legs to himself. He catches your eyes— *Let's try again*—moves his feet slowly, much more slowly than the beat of the music. Back, forward, side side, back, side, his dark dry hands on your upper arms. *Bien, sí, bien.* He slinks and slides and you move faster together until you are blushing with pleasure. Finally, it is you who pushes up to Ramón, spreading your legs a little, letting him take a bit of your weight because now you trust him not to drop or mock you. You have the rhythm, his thigh under yours, when the sky opens up and the foam begins to fall. Everyone cheers and raises their arms and faces up while it falls and falls, the soap bubbles breaking up the dance floor lights like a thousand prisms, catching in braids and eyelashes, tickling your lips until you are knee deep in clouds. When it is finally done, Ramón turns to you, smiling wide, his hand still on your arm, and lifts his finger to dab foam onto your nose.

When you and María finally go home, Manny is nowhere to be found and you leave without saying goodbye.

"Burros!"

You and María have come home past curfew. Your shoes and socks are wet with foam. Gabi is in a knee-length pajama shirt with Tweetie on the front and her feet are bare. Her toenails are thick with red nail polish and her black and gray hair is pulled back in a scrunchy.

"Ustedes son burros!" Gabi makes María lean forward and smells her breath.

"Cerveza!" Gabi points a short finger at María and María vigorously denies it. Then Gabi insists on smelling your breath. You haven't been drinking but you are sure you smell like it. The dance club was sticky with spilled beer and thick with cigarette smoke. Gabi can't decide about you, trusts you. She asks you what you've been doing, who María has been dancing with. You say you haven't been drinking, which isn't a lie. When she asks about *hombres*, you say that you and María danced with the whole group at once. *Todos amigos*. For the first time you pretend to understand less than you do. You keep your answers vague and you can't tell if Gabi believes you.

When Gabi finally goes back to bed, María gives you a hug and giggles, a little drunk. "Gracias," she says.

María gets some water from the kitchen and shuts the door to her room, leaving you the last one in the living room. You turn out the light. In the dark, the angels seem to glow *at* you and you worry that you are doing the wrong thing. But you've always been loyal to friends, or mostly, never had a friend need much more than a white lie. You remember once, when you were twelve, how your friend stole a lipstick from a convenience store and you used it with her in the bathroom afterward and laughed. How when you were eight you lied and said your little brother had broken a picture frame, and your parents had known you were lying and you were in trouble for a week. How at fifteen you told a girl a friend's secret to impress her, but that girl didn't even seem to care. You feel bad about all these things, but also like you deserve credit for the things you have thought of and not done. The lies you haven't told. The fun you haven't had.

You aren't sure why María isn't supposed to date, and Anselmo seems nice, and she's older than you, which means she must know what she's doing. You touch the ceramic angel with the broken wing for good luck and feel a little better. Your superstition is getting worse.

When you stumble into the bathroom, eager to brush your teeth and fall into bed, you are startled to see a stranger's face in the mirror, a girl covered with black eyeliner and sweat. You aren't sure how to get the makeup off.

III.

"We're taking you somewhere special," Ramón says in Spanish, but he won't tell you where because it's a surprise. María and the boys climb into Ramón's VW Beetle with a sun roof carved from the ceiling. Manny is the last to arrive, smelling like bread, flour on his shoes. You sit in the front seat, on María's lap, and try to protest when Jorge in the back seat puts his hands over the driver's eyes and they play *pollo*, chicken. No, no, you say, but no one is listening, everyone is laughing, and for a moment you think you may actually die on this, your last night in Pachuca.

In twenty-four hours you will be home and this place, this cramped bug with no seatbelts, will seem as far away, as inconceivable, as Minnesota does right now. There is no more time to wait for Manny to make the move; you will have to kiss him. Even as you think this, your stomach clenches. You are comforted by the thought that no matter what happens, you will be gone.

It's only a short drive, through a part of the city that is more familiar now, past the movie theater and a dark row of buildings with tall fences around their parking lots. Then the car pulls over onto a dirt lot and stops. Everyone piles out. The lot is dark and empty and you can't tell why you're there, though everyone else seems to know, since they all head for a fence and begin hopping over it. You stick by Manny so that he is the one to help you over. He takes your hand; it is warm and yours is cold. You don't like climbing fences. This one is about a foot taller than you, with wire mesh that is barely wide enough to fit the toe of your sneaker. At the top, you hesitate, then jump down, landing hard, not light like the boys do.

Over the fence is an empty amusement park. At first,

all you can see is the Ferris wheel looming above the rest of the black shapes, lit from behind by the glow of the city. Then, as your eyes adjust, you see a Tilt-a-Whirl and a log flume and booths covered with canvas for games and food. The park is a bit dilapidated—with trash on the ground and a smell like wet dog even though it hasn't rained recently—but not so decayed that it might not be guarded by someone.

"Donde estamos?" you ask, nervous but fascinated.

"La Disneylandía de México," Ramón says and everyone bursts into laughter. You laugh too, but you don't feel in on the joke. Are they laughing at you or at themselves or at a world that can contain so many different places all at once?

María and Anselmo quickly split off from the group to make out in one of the unmoving Tilt-a-Whirl seats. You watch them go, a little anxious and a little jealous. Since the dance, they've gone off alone together more and more. Instead of going out with the group, you and María have gone to the movies, María leaving you in the third row to sit in the back with Anselmo. Sometimes you turn to look for her in the flickering dark, and you think maybe she isn't there at all, that she's left you, and you feel a rise of that fear from those first days in Pachuca. That you are alone. That you've made a mistake. You've hardly seen Manny. You tell yourself that this is what growing up is, this pairing off, these unspoken contracts between friends, but since you're lying for her, you wish she would tell you more, include you, confide in you, so that you can feel older, so that you can better share the blame.

Everyone else follows Ramón. It's as if the fact that the car is his makes him the temporary leader of the group. You feel that somehow this park is *his* place.

"Te gusta?" Ramón asks.

"Sí. Claro," you say, though you still aren't sure what you're being asked to like.

Ramón smiles.

"Is it abandoned?" you ask in Spanish.

You can have a conversation. You still butcher the grammar and there are many words you don't know (*Mande? What?*) but you can hear where the slippery words are joined, where the *s*'s are dropped or the words elided. Ramón tells you the park isn't abandoned, just closed until someone with money decides to open it again. He says that they come here often, to drink or smoke, to talk into the night, to bring *mujeres para una noche romántica*. Even though you change your pace, try walking slow, then fast, then turning to talk to the other boys, Ramón sticks by your side, pointing to objects and naming them, *pochoclo, basura, juegos,* as if this amusement park requires a tour guide.

Past the closed booths and behind a giant slide is a carousel, and that is where everyone stops. Ramón sits on a black horse, Manny on a white tiger, and you sit between them on a green dragon with a curling tail. Jorge and Luis both sit on brown horses. Skinny, tall Luis folds up like a paperclip; Jorge looks relaxed sitting sidesaddle.

"Que linda," you say, because it really is beautiful. In the dark, the animals of the carousel and the paintings on the ceiling and walls seem alive.

"Cuídate," Manny says, *be careful*, and he tells a story about a stray dog they found in the park one night who was nosing through some trash looking for food. When Luis tried to feed him, the dog snarled and bit his hand.

"What a disgusting dinner you would be," Jorge says, and you laugh, since Ramón and Luis are laughing, but now you worry that every movement in the shadows is a hungry, bruised animal. Pachuca is full of these strays, their coats thin and patchy.

The boys talk and you listen, focusing hard and understanding most of what they say. After a while, you start to zone out, too tired to pay attention anymore. When you go back to Minnesota, you will be startled by all that you can understand without even listening, and for a while you will be unable *not* to eavesdrop.

Your mind, unused to tuning out English, will be pelted with conversation.

"Me muero por una cheve," Manny says, lighting a cigarette, and everyone agrees.

There's beer in the trunk of the bug. Manny slides off the white tiger.

"I'll help you," you say and the boys look surprised. Maybe they can hear your heart pounding. "I've never had a drink in Disneyland," you say, and you try to sound casual, flip.

"Una cheve por la gringa!" Finally their little *mascota* is going to have a drink.

Walking back, your eyes used to the dark, the park seems much smaller, and soon Manny is helping you back over the fence. His hand is still warm, yours is now clammy.

The bug isn't locked. The car is too old, and fixing the locks would cost more than the whole thing is worth. You stand close to Manny as he reaches into the trunk and pulls out a couple of sweating liter bottles. Now, you think, now, but you have no idea what to do. How can you kiss him when he's a moving target? You are angry that he won't stand still. Then you could look him in the eyes and maybe he'd bend down and kiss you and you wouldn't have to be the one to do it. Then you would know that he wants it too.

But no, it has to be you. You are walking back toward the fence, holding one of the bottles. The moment almost gone, you take his hand to hop the fence and squeeze and don't let go or move to climb. He looks at you and smiles and then ruffles your hair as if you're a little girl.

"You are bad at climbing fences," he says.

"I know," you say, and still you don't move to climb.

"You can't let the fence know you're afraid."

You take it as a sign.

He's still looking at you and you lift up onto your toes, moving your mouth toward his, afraid to close your eyes because you'll miss his mouth, end up kissing his chin or his nose. Because your eyes are open, you see the moment he realizes what you are trying to do, the moment he turns toward the fence, pretending that he hasn't noticed, that you are on your tiptoes to begin climbing.

"I can't do it with the beer," you say, happy your voice sounds steady. You hand him the bottle, then climb without his hand helping you up. On the other side of the fence, you say, "I'm going to find María," and walk away before he has a chance to follow you. Your eyes feel hot and full and you try to blink away tears, to control your humiliation. If you cry, everyone will know what happened.

You look for María on the Tilt-a-Whirl but she isn't there. Maybe she is back with the group. But even as you think it, you know it isn't true. You know she is somewhere with Anselmo and you know they are having sex and the thought of their bodies moving together brings a feeling of panic deep into your lungs, like asthma or a drag on a cigarette and you want to find her but you don't want to see with your eyes what you can see in your mind because you are a coward. And maybe that is why you have never been kissed. Maybe this scared little girl is who you will be for the rest of your life.

You walk away from the Tilt-a-Whirl, away from the carousel, until you come to the Ferris wheel. You are a climber of fences now. You jump the rails instead of walking through the snaking, empty line. A car sits at the bottom of the wheel, and you step from the platform into it, startled when the car swings a little. You tuck your legs under you, afraid to let them dangle in case there are any feral dogs living in the darkness below the wheel, and then you look up. It is a clear night and you can see the stars through the metal framework. You wish the wheel was working so that you could go to the top.

As you sit, the pressure behind your eyes slowly eases. *None of this matters. It isn't even real. Tomorrow it will be gone*. And you are afraid that may be true. Soon, you'll be able to head back to the group. Pretend you are fine until you are.

"Gringa."

You start so hard the cart jerks with you. Ramón hops the rails and you scoot over. He sits down next to you.

"Todo bien?" he asks. He's been looking for you.

"I didn't want a beer after all," you say.

He nods, as if it is a good reason to be hiding here. "Good choice. That beer was warm."

The two of you sit quietly.

"I need to find María," you say.

"I'm sure she's fine," Ramón says and he turns to you and takes your hand.

When he puts his mouth on yours, his lips are dry like his hands. He opens his mouth a little, and you open yours, and you taste the beer on his tongue and wonder if you should be carried away. Already, you are trying to remember this differently. To frame it into the story you want to tell, as if Manny had never existed, as if looking up through the Ferris wheel into the sky felt like looking through the heart of the Eiffel Tower. You linger on his mouth, unsure how to tell when a kiss is over.

———

In the morning, it is Ramón who picks you up and takes you, Gabi, and María to the airport. His bug seems spacious with only the four of you inside. Gabi talks incessantly, firing questions at you, and even though you'd rather be quiet, you feel like you have to respond. María has been quiet all morning, a little sad, and Gabi thinks that it is because María will miss you and you wonder if that is true. Out the window, Pachuca rolls by, then green fields, small towns, and finally the outer slums of Mexico City. Shacks that look like they are made with apple crates, roads that are muddy and rutted. Then you are at the airport.

Ramón takes your suitcase from the trunk and surprises you with flowers. You blush, say *gracias*, and wonder if you ought to kiss him again, if once you have kissed someone you are obliged to continue, if he expects you to, and once you frame it this way, like a chore, you cannot remember if you wanted to kiss him again. You give him a hug. Then you hug María, then Gabi, who is crying loudly and saying she will miss you. You wonder who will have to dust the angels now.

You walk to the security checkpoint and when you get to the front of the line, put your carryon on the conveyor belt, the security guard gestures to the flowers. "No," he says, and at first you don't understand what he means. No, you can't go home. No, you aren't done here. "You can't take plants from Mexico into the United States." You step out of line, holding the flowers in front of you, unsure what to do.

Finally, it's María who steps forward. She takes a few flowers out of the bouquet. "One for each of us," she says as she leans in and gives you a tight hug. Before you can think of something to say, she is walking away.

You smile at the group one last time, and then you turn and drop the remaining flowers into the wastebasket. It isn't until you are on the plane that you find the crushed head of a purple lilac slipped into your pocket.

FOR A GOOD TIME, CALL

The wrong numbers were always men and they always asked for Gail. When Megan said she wasn't Gail, didn't know anyone named Gail, some stuttered apologies, some insisted she *was* Gail or that Gail was nearby. Some wanted to talk to her about the fickleness of women. Yes, she agreed, Gail seemed to be a bitch. Yes, it was cruel to give out a fake number. Yes, dating was hard. No, it was never okay to use the word "cunt." *Don't answer the phone*, the boyfriend said, but Megan was applying for jobs and every time the phone rang, her heart seized with hope. She'd run from the bathroom, pants unzipped; fumble in her purse while driving; risk life and limb and so forth. And even after she got a new job, a job she liked even less than the old one, she kept answering. She could never resist an unknown number.

One hungover morning, the boyfriend broke up with her. That night, she drank a bottle of wine and reactivated her OkCupid profile. The only thing that had changed was her age, from thirty-one to thirty-two, and the fact that she hadn't loved him—

She answered the phone.

"Gail's dead," she said. She sounded believable, the way Gail's sister might sound, heartbroken, now burdened with answering the phone after Gail's tragic accident. A car crash? Bungee-jumping? She didn't know anything about Gail's interests.

"Oh, my god," said the man on the phone. "Oh my god."

He sounded so genuinely distressed that she felt bad.

"Not really," she said. "I don't know Gail. This is a wrong number."

The man paused, as if waiting for an explanation. "That's fucked up, lady," he said. Then he hung up.

There was no reason for him to be upset. She'd been trying to spare him the pain of rejection. Why did he want Gail anyway? Was Gail special? Megan had spent hours imagining Gail, at first as a pathetic ditz who couldn't get her own phone number right, who sat home alone and wondered why no one ever called. Then she pictured Gail as a married woman, a desperate flirt never brave enough to close the deal. Now she wondered where Gail met all these men. Gail, she worried as she painted her big toe Tattle Teal blue, was having a lot more fun than she was.

Later that night, after she'd fallen asleep on the couch, she got another call.

"'lo?" she said.

"Oh god, I woke you up. I'm sorry."

"No, it's fine. I wasn't asleep."

The man didn't contradict her, but she could tell he was skeptical.

"I had fun last night."

"Who is this?"

"It's Richard. Richard from last night. You gave me your number." He paused again. "Look, I'm sorry I woke you up."

"I was awake."

"Right. Well, I was calling to say it was nice to meet you, and would you like to have dinner on Friday?"

"Dinner," she said. "Okay."

When she woke up, she had to check to make sure she hadn't dreamed it.

They met at seven at a Mexican restaurant in Pacific Beach. She was in her favorite dress, a short black thing that hugged her breasts but not her hips. She was fifteen minutes early and every time a man walked up to the restaurant alone, she said, "Richard?" The first three men she stopped were wrong. Then, at seven sharp, a man with salt and pepper hair stopped outside the door. He was older than she'd expected, probably forty, and wearing a suit. She revised her assessment of Gail. Maybe Gail was someone who picked up sugar daddies, flirted some drinks off them, then "had a headache," or simply disappeared, slipping out to meet a younger, hotter guy—the guy she actually wanted.

The man began pacing, stopped to adjust his tie, then checked his phone. His eyes flicked over her without a second glance. This new idea of Gail made Megan feel self-conscious, old even though he was older. The kind of woman he didn't look at twice.

"Richard?" she said.

"Yes?" He ran his hand through his hair.

"It's Gail."

He looked at her more closely, his thick eyebrows drawing together in a squint. She wondered if he usually wore glasses.

"You look different," he said.

"Do I?"

"You seem shorter and your hair isn't blond."

"Wasn't parking a nightmare?"

She watched as he thought about saying something more. He ran his hand through his hair again. "Sorry," he said. "Pacific Beach is always crowded on the weekend." Then he opened the door for her.

To start, she ordered a frozen margarita with salt.

"The same," he said, and smiled. He was a pleaser.

"So, what do you do?" she asked.

"I'm a dentist. Remember?"

"We were both drunk," she said, and flicked her wrist as if to say, who can remember what happened that long ago, when we were different people? The margaritas arrived and she took a sip. "I always have cavities, but I brush twice a day, floss. Why is that?"

"Some people have bad genes," he said. "Me, I brush twice a day, floss, prescription fluoride mouthwash, I still have cavities. My ex-wife, she brushed once a day, max. Never needed anything but a cleaning."

She nodded. There were some people who were like that—people to whom things came easily.

"Do you believe in love, Richard?"

"Yes?" he said.

"I don't," she said. "Because love doesn't need to be

believed in. It just is, without needing us. It doesn't need us at all. That is what I don't like about love."

"I figured you'd want me to say yes," he said.

"Then you don't believe in love?"

"No, I guess I still do. I mean, there isn't love without people to be in love, right?"

"But if we make it, shouldn't it be like jungle gyms or pancakes? I can make a pancake, but when I do, I don't need to believe in the pancake. And the pancake doesn't *poof* turn into an omelet, or something you don't like at all, like tuna fish salad."

"I like tuna fish salad," he said.

When her chilaquiles came, they weren't very good. She should have known better. It was a dish best ordered in restaurants where soccer was always on, where the TV was in the corner of the ceiling, small and high so the men who watched had to huddle together and crane their necks as if in prayer. This restaurant had a huge TV over the bar, an HD mega-whatever that showed the hair on the back of the baseball players' necks. She picked at the food.

"What are we going to do?" he said after the waiter took away their plates.

"Fuck?"

"No, about the bill."

"Oh. I guess we'll split it."

After dinner they took a walk west down Garnet, toward the water, passing tourist shops and bead stores
and an ice-cream parlor she hadn't been to in years.
Even from the sidewalk, it smelled like butter, butter
mixed with the ocean, which smelled like salt, but not
only salt. The ocean smelled like fish and wet hair and
the vegetable drawer in her refrigerator that she cleaned
only when something rotted.

They walked until they got to the boardwalk, and
then they took the smooth concrete steps down to the
water. The tide was going out, slowly exposing the wet
wooden poles of the pier, looming dark over their left
shoulders. To the north the shore curved almost imper-
ceptibly, until it curled on the edge of the horizon into a
cove where the lights of La Jolla were nestled.

"I love the ocean," she said.

"Me too," he said.

"I prefer the ocean at night," she said.

"I'm a morning person," he said.

They took their shoes off, and he offered to carry
hers, but she worried they smelled and said no. They
picked their way along the stretch of smooth dark sand
that low tide had strewn with seaweed, pebbles, and the
occasional abandoned crab, searching for the water.

"I wish the moon were full," she said. "We could look for sand dollars. When they first wash ashore, they aren't hard yet. They dry in the sun." She'd collected them as a kid, patiently searching the shoreline for bleached, brittle bodies, no one competing with her, rushing her. Her mother had helped her glue them onto an old cigar box, a place to keep her jewelry.

"You know I'm not Gail, right?" she said.

"I suppose I do," he said. "It doesn't make that much of a difference to me."

"What did you like about Gail?"

He dug his toes into the cold wet sand. They were too long to be handsome.

"She was easy to talk to, I guess," he said. "And we were drunk, we talked a lot, the way people do. I woke up the next day hoping I hadn't said too much."

"What did you say?"

"I was drunk. I'm not drunk now."

"Pretend." She kicked a little sand at him. If he could tell Gail, he could tell her too.

"I don't know," he said. "It's hard to remember. I'm divorced. I talked about my ex-wife."

"I don't want to hear about her," she said.

"Sure. Well, Gail was divorced too, we had that in common. I told her I hadn't had sex in a year, since the divorce. She said it was no big deal." He paused, waiting perhaps for Megan to say the same, then shrugged. "But then she gave me your number."

She took his hand, and they started walking again. If Gail was divorced, she couldn't be a hot young twenty-something. Maybe Gail was like this man, still good looking but nervous about getting older. She wondered why Gail hadn't wanted Richard for herself. Maybe Gail was too picky. Maybe she gave every man she met Megan's number, because she was afraid.

"Is Gail beautiful?" she asked.

"I don't remember," he said. "I suppose I thought so. Why?"

"No reason. Just curious."

When they arrived at their cars, she invited him to follow her back to her place for a drink. Thrumming down the freeway, she turned up the radio and listened to songs from high school, each one grooved into her memory. She used to always drive like this—both windows down, the music so loud it pushed back at the wind. When she sang, she could not hear herself. When she put her arm out the window, the air made her wrist dance, and it felt wonderful, to be powerful and powerless.

At her apartment, she poured them white wine, which they drank too quickly, and then they each drank another glass, a little slower. Richard was patient and she was surprised to be nervous. When they kissed, she could tell that he would never be an amazing kisser, but his lips were gentle and he held onto her, and that was what she wanted. When they walked into her bedroom, she put her hand on his chest.

"I'm Megan," she said, and she wished it was the confession of a secret identity, instead of a condition from which she might never recover.

NAKANO TAKEKO IS FATALLY SHOT, JAPAN, 1868

My sister Yūko carries my head in her hands, looking for a place to bury it. Me here in her arms and me a woman on the field with a bullet wound that has ceased to bleed. The Imperial Army will carry away a corpse, but they will not have me for a trophy.

I say to my sister with my last breath, *you must cut off my head*. Then I die, so she cannot argue.

The guillotine is a humane invention—there is no pain, they say. The blade falls fast and clean. But it is too easy to let gravity take the task into its own hands. There is always more gravity and we will make baskets until our fingers bleed from weaving. Anyone can release a blade. There is only honor in the kill that kills a little bit of the self.

I have killed men by cutting their throats, death accomplished in a single blow. To sever a head is different. It requires hatred, a mania that cuts through the skin and muscle and hacks through the bone, that covers hands in blood, to prove oneself master of the body of the dead, to prove that the body is dead dead dead.

To keep to her task, Yūko hates. She will love me again, but never in the same way. I have asked for something which can never be completely forgiven.

I will not do this, my sister says, holding my dead body to her chest.

Yūko buries me at the foot of a pine tree and I am almost at peace. I am as the other seeds that fall here, too close to their mother to take root and so reconciled to lie in her shade until they rot. Yūko lies on the ground above where she has buried me and spreads her arms wide. She presses her face to the freshly turned soil. I long to hold her back but I must wait. I wait and wait until I am part of the earth again, my hair tangled with the roots of the pine tree, my arms the arms of gravity, the gravity we use to kill, yes, but now I use it to hold my sister as tight and gentle as when we were children, spinning her around, and though she feels nothing, I know we are still playing.

I will not do this, she says, but it is done.

INISHMORE

Halfway up the steep hill, we rest on a jutting slab of limestone. Lacy sits at the edge, dangling her legs over the five-foot drop, her long paisley skirt taut across her thighs. I sit cross-legged a few feet back; I've never liked heights, even heights so un-high that Lacy says I'm *afraid of shorts*. Up high everything feels untrustworthy. Stone could crack. My body, mistaking thought for command, could act out my imagined falling—and I always imagine falling. Lacy knows this. When we were little, she tormented me by hanging upside-down off the top bunk, her long ponytail swinging like a bell pull. *Look at me. Look, Andrea.*

I wait for her to tease me now, but she doesn't. We're being careful with each other, keeping our conversations small. Lacy grabs a bag of M&Ms out of our day-pack and pours them out into her skirt. She picks out the reds, hands them to me, then divides out the oranges for herself. Eating through the rainbow, an old ritual to bargain with the world: it's a gesture of peace.

This tension is my fault: I woke her up this morning, she hid under the hostel's scratchy wool blanket, and it was like a switch flipped: we are fourteen and sixteen again, late for school, Dad asleep on the couch from drinking, Mom long gone to her hospital shift, me in charge, the car running in the driveway, defrost melting ice off the windshield until under the ice a layer of water forms, until you can break ice off in large chunks, like picking a scab. *I'm leaving without you*, I yell, wanting her to think I'd do it, half-believing I might. I never get farther than the next block. And then this morning there she was in bed, turned from me, and this switch flipped and I was a *bitch*. I knew I was being a bitch, acting crazy, and I watched me watch myself, thinking, why aren't you stepping in to calm yourself down? but I didn't *want* to, angry enough that I slapped the pillow next to her head, wishing I could yank her out of bed by her hair. When she sat up and asked what the fuck was wrong with me, I had no answer.

Now I pop an M&M into my mouth. My palm is stained red. I want to apologize again, tell her that I know we're grownups, that no one is supposed to be in charge anymore. *Then don't be*, Lacy would say.

"My shoes are still wet," I say instead. It has rained for four days straight and our packs smell like mold, our damp clothes hang limp from our bunk bed, bras and underwear flutter shameless in the draft.

"You shouldn't tuck them under yourself like that. Sun them." She kicks her own feet through the air to demonstrate.

I stick my legs straight out in front of me and my heels jut over the edge, my muddy toes superimposed over the narrow dirt road that cuts from one side of the island to the other. Above us is a ruin of an old monastery, mostly a jumble of rocks. We'll climb what's left of its walls, then hike back to the hostel. Tomorrow morning we'll visit Dun Aengus, then catch the ferry back to Galway, stay there a few nights, and end our trip in Dublin. The Guinness factory, Temple Bar, Glendalough. I tick them off, the plans I've made, the hostels, buses, plane flights, food budget, a litany to finish. This trip was something that, as college ended, *could* be planned, then executed. Off with its head. Too soon I'll be back in my old room, parents asleep down the hall tangled in their own problems, everything the same like I never left. I'm afraid I'll forget that I ever have. That's the thing about places you know too well, and people—there's an old-self waiting to take you back, to sneak up behind you and clap a formaldehyde-soaked cloth to your mouth before you know to scream. When I am home, I keep a lookout; I keep my back to the wall.

This is how my thoughts unspool, like a line with a fish, hissing out downstream. I am an experienced fisherwoman. I can reel in my line. Today is where I am. The ground is wet; it sweats. The rock remains unsplit beneath my long thighs. Friday night is disco night at Joe Watty's pub. Patrick and Leo who work at the hostel are taking us.

Lacy hands me the yellow M&Ms.

"Patrick's cute," I say.

"Patrick *is* cute." Lacy turns to look at me. "Leo thinks Patrick likes you."

"Whatever," I say. She waits for me to say more, and I want to, but that stubbornness rises in me that I call being private, but is mostly fear that if I express what I want I'll jinx it, or almost as bad, be embarrassed. After the silence has gone on long enough, she brushes M&M shells off her skirt and stands so quickly that I tell her to be careful of the edge before I can stop myself.

Waiting for the rain to end, we'd done nothing but play Scrabble with Reba. The hostel's board was ancient. It flopped limply apart at its fold, the tiles yellowed like old teeth. Every day, after they finished cleaning up breakfast, sweeping the cracks in the floorboards, Patrick and Leo joined us.

Reba is sixty and English. She wears a floral handkerchief over her long gray-brown hair and her skin is starting to become loose beneath her arms and chin. She came to Inishmore once in the seventies, before there were reliable ferries for tourists. A man took her out here in a rowboat. He didn't charge her anything, but he did make her row for a spell while he ate a sandwich and drank dark beer from a thermos. At the time, she tells us, pinching the letter *A* between her thin fingers, there were no hostels. She moved from family to family, helping people haul seaweed to the pastures that make the whole island look like a patchwork quilt, small fields stitched together with low limestone walls. "People have been hauling seaweed out of the ocean, layering it with sand to make the soil, since before Christ." That is Reba's way of talking. Slow and soft, with gravity and a sense of time. She paid a little money for rent when people asked for it and she cooked sometimes. "Simple stuff," she said. "Potatoes mostly." She was on the island for a year.

It must have rained a lot the last time she was on the island because she knows all the two letter Scrabble words: *ab*, *fa*, *fe*, *xi*, *xu*, *ya*, *za*. There are a million of these bullshit words. She beat us all so badly that we changed the rules: no words you can't define *without* looking them up. And even that didn't help. She played *yo* (sweetheart), *ka* (spirit), and *qi* (the vital force in Chinese thought). What that vital force was she wasn't sure, but we counted it. Thirty-three points for the triple word score. As we sat around the board, stared at the afternoon rain running down the warped-glass windows, drank the beer that Patrick and Leo had made in the claw-foot bathtub, we debated what *qi* might be.

"It's like air or something," Lacy said.

"Gravity," I said.

"Qi. K-wheee." Leo lay on his back, blowing cigarette smoke at the ceiling. "It's like what's in weed. Whatsit. THC."

"You're an idiot," Patrick said. Patrick has green eyes and shoulders thin as wishbones. I imagine grabbing him, pushing back on his shoulders until he snaps at the sternum, opening him to the wind. We sat on the floor with our knees nearly touching.

"Qi is like that stuff that holds the muscle to the bone," Reba said. Lacy turned toward her in appreciation.

"Deep," Leo said.

I would like Reba more if Lacy liked her less. It's this side of Lacy I don't know: this long-skirt wearing, co-op living, Beloit girl who wears her hair in a long, simple braid down her back. Not the Lacy who couldn't save more than ten dollars at a time because there was always a new shirt, a new color of nail polish, because a boyfriend needed it and she's a generous person, easy with people in the way I'm not. For this trip, she saved two thousand dollars. Her nails are trimmed neat and short. She's quieter, but she and Reba like to talk. When the rain let up a little, they went to look at the garden out back, Leo went to check on the stew, and Patrick said he couldn't stand to be inside for another minute. We went out and stood under the tin awning of the hostel, looking out over the fields of walls.

"I love it here," I said. His hand was at that uncomfortable distance—near enough to reach for, but still separate, motionless as if unaware of any danger from clammy me. Afraid I'd make a grab for him, I held my own hand instead. Patrick stubbed out his cigarette on a rock from before Christ and went back inside.

When we were little, we fought: pinching, kicking, slapping, biting (Lacy). When she tried to hit me, I held her arms at her sides and she would howl, "Stop it. Stop it. Stop it."

"Are you going to keep hitting me?" I'd ask and she'd

set her teeth, hissing, and throw her body from side to side. When I did let go, her arms would fly up to my chest to be caught again, until I got frustrated and ended the fight with one slap across her face. Those fights taught me what it meant to be bigger than someone else.

One summer, when she was eight and I was ten, we'd been fighting about I don't remember what, but I know I'd ended it, because Lacy was on the floor crying while I tried to quiet her. Dad was down in the basement. "Shh," I said. "You're okay. You're okay." Of course he heard us, I see now he probably always heard us, but this day, for whatever reason, he yelled, "Girls! Down here now," in that tone he had. The one that said, *you are in real shit.* We slunk downstairs. He sat at his carving table, bent over a block of wood that would someday mirror the bookend he'd already finished: a deer leaping out of grass, as if something in the books had startled it. He was drinking a beer, the Twins game on the radio next to him.

He didn't acknowledge us right away, making us wait, until Lacy blurted out "She hit me," as I said, "It wasn't my fault."

"Both of you, shut up." He turned to us, pointing at me and then her with the neck of his beer bottle. Our father, when he was angry, wielded pauses. His silence more frightening than his yell, the suspense worse than anything. We had seen him, waiting for the right words to come, slam cabinets hard enough to break dishes. He paused for so long, I was afraid he expected us to speak, to say something that could only be wrong.

"Sisters don't rat each other out," he said. "You go upstairs, make up, and I don't *ever* want to hear the two of you fighting again. Is that clear?" We nodded. "You only get one sister," he said and we wanted him to say more, that he missed his older brother, an uncle we rarely saw, a man even more mysterious than our father. We liked to imagine what we never believed: that this uncle would someday come to our home with a wife and children, an extended family to make holidays boisterous and our father happy. But Dad bent back over his work. His knife nicked off a flake of wood, the ear of the deer emerging. "Don't fuck it up. Not everyone is as lucky as you two."

When we got to the top of the stairs, out of sight of our father, Lacy slipped her hand into mine. We went outside and played Lacy's favorite game, runaway orphan warrior princesses, which I usually pretended I was too old for but that day I didn't. We roamed our cul-de-sac, rescuing each other from prisons made of hedges and avoiding the gaze of the dragon (Mrs. Hendrick's terrier, who sat in her window and barked if it saw you) until the streetlights came on and we had to go home.

———

Getting ready to go to the pub, the night seems ripe with possibility. Everyone feels it, the end of the rain like a blessing. Lacy and I are ebullient; we giggle and sniff our armpits, clean our cheeks with Wet Wipes, and share what's left in our bottle of concealer. We've tanned on our travels, and the concealer leaves a faint peach moon under our chins that we try to smudge with fingers and spit. When Reba walks in on us still in our bras, Lacy squeals and pretends to be embarrassed. I pretend not to be. She asks Reba if she wants to come with us.

Reba just smiles. "I'll pour you into bed when you come home," she says.

"We'll miss you," Lacy says, and I don't know if it is the sunshine or the M&Ms or the fact that we are here, at this moment, and our distance from home feels like a miracle we've performed, but I'm happy enough to nod in agreement and almost mean it.

Patrick and Leo come with us, Leo teasing that without them, we'd be lost. Only one road passes the hostel, dirt and wide, and we turn left, downhill, toward the port at Kilronan. Impossible to get lost; also, it turns out, impossible to miss the pub, which is by itself half a mile later, a yellow sign and nothing but field on either side. Inside, we sit at a little four top and Patrick goes to buy us drinks. Behind us on the wall is an advertisement for Guinness. *Guinness Is Good for You!* says a large, presumably intoxicated cartoon toucan. We drink one round, Leo buys the second. At ten, the lights go out, a spot hits a disco ball, and the Irish folk music is replaced by Diana Ross.

"Come on," Patrick says, and he holds out his hand. Leo offers his hand to Lacy and she smiles and stands, but keeps her fingers resting on her skirt. It makes me feel obvious, reaching for Patrick. Leo flirts with Lacy but they stay a solid foot apart on the dance floor. Patrick pulls me close. I'm a pretty good dancer but my hiking boots make me feel like I'm dancing in concrete blocks. I put my hands on his forearms; they are as impossibly thin as they look, but strong. I couldn't break him open if I tried.

We dance.

Patrick finds out I've never had a baby Guinness and buys four of them. A shot of Kahlua with Irish cream on top, it looks like a tiny, froth-topped stout. Lacy and I both take two gulps to get ours down and afterward my spit is sweet, my tongue plays over the grit left on my teeth. I'm drunk. Four weeks of hiking, of sharing sandwiches, has made me a lightweight. When Leo buys another round of beers I hold mine cautiously, like it's a baby or a vase. Can't spill a drop.

When Lacy and I go to the bathroom, I promise Patrick that I will be *right back*. I put my hand on his chest, as if I'm reassuring him. *Right back*.

"I'm drunk," I say, leaning against the bathroom wall. People have written on it like a yearbook. *Mary and Glenn '98. drunk octopus was here. ~~your~~ you're ~~beautiful stupid~~ a potato. G&P BFFs 4ever. and that has made all the difference.*

Lacy nods. "I didn't mean to get drunk," she says, like she's surprised to find herself wearing mismatched socks. I wonder if Lacy has been drunk before. Not flush-faced and voluble—*Am I drunk? I think I'm drunk*—but the kind of drunk where you scare yourself, where it comes on suddenly, and you know you need to leave, to vomit and hide and wait out the things you've done to yourself. Lacy must have gotten that drunk, but then we've never talked much about drinking, and Dad wasn't that kind of drunk anyway. He approached his oblivion with quiet determination.

I bet a lot of people have pressed forehead to porcelain in this bathroom.

"We just won't drink anymore," I say. "If we see the other person drinking more, we'll tell them, no more drinking more."

She nods again, this time at our excellent plan. "Do you have a pen?" she asks.

I wish that I did. I'd like to make a mark here. "What would you write?" I ask.

Lacy looks at the wall, takes her time, runs her fingers over the warped paint, the cartoon cocks and balls, Gandhi quotes, the many different scrawls that link letters into words. There doesn't seem to be much left to say on the subject of Inishmore, love, travel, or life. "Blank walls say nothing," she says.

I can't tell if she wants to write that, or if she's stating a fact.

"Do you want to go back to the hostel soon?" she asks. "I really *am* drunk."

I should be the big sister and take her home, but isn't that exactly what Lacy doesn't want me to be? I don't want to go back yet. Patrick is waiting for me. "We'll go back soon," I say.

An hour later I've finished my beer, but this one is definitely my last. The room pulses with music and the humid air has passed through too many lungs; there's no oxygen left. Lacy and Leo dance more closely now. Patrick says he wants some fresh air and though I know what that means and I have been wavering all night— kiss him, don't kiss him, fuck his brains out and disappear without a trace—when he heads for the door, I follow. Behind the pub, we sit on a low wall. The air draws goose bumps from my sweaty skin.

"I love it here," I say. That seems to be the only thing I can say to Patrick.

Patrick turns out to be a good kisser.

We kiss for a long time. Or it feels like a long time. He has a hand on my thigh. Then the other is under my shirt and pulling my bra down and I let him even though it's light enough near the pub that anyone could see us. My hands stay rested on his shoulders, touching the hair at his nape, until he picks one up and moves it to his crotch, presses it down and up a few times, lets go when he seems to think I've got the hang of it. I am aroused. I am frightened. I wish I'd already made this choice back in the pub, back in the hostel, because right now it seems important to know if I plan to fuck him or blow him or leave him hard and a bit led on. I'm not sure I want to be doing this and don't see why I wouldn't want to do it except that when I imagine his hand in my hair, pressing my face to his lap, I need more air than his kiss allows and pull away.

"Everything all right?" he whispers, and strokes my hair.

"I'm pretty drunk," I say. Above me, for the first time since we arrived on the island, there are no clouds and I can see the stars, thick like milk, like whole milk spilled on granite, and then there are too many and I have to close my eyes against them, but still the constellations on my eyelids spin and swoop.

"We're so small and big," I say, my head on his shoulder. He starts kissing my ear, then my neck, then he's turning me toward him again. "We'll be getting busy soon," he says, and he must mean sex, but then he says, "Do you speak any other languages?"

"Not really," I say.

"Think about it." He bites my earlobe a touch too hard and kisses me again, before I can ask what, exactly, I am meant to be thinking. When he ends the kiss, he holds my shoulders and smiles at me like I've done something very right. I smile back.

"I need to take Lacy home," I say, though what I mean is, I want the night to stop here, when everything is perfect. We stand to go back inside and I stumble. When he puts his hand at the small of my back, it feels right to have him guiding me.

In the case of worldwide apocalypse, when the major cities have been knocked out and all communications go down, Lacy and I have decided to meet in Iowa City,

Iowa, in the cemetery, at the statue of the Black Angel. The statue will be easy to find and the city, we feel, is unlikely to be targeted because there isn't much going on. Then, because we are in the middle of the country, we can travel in any direction, depending on the specific circumstances of the apocalypse.

This plan, this kind of worst-case worrying, smacks of me but it was Lacy who called late at night my freshman year of college. She'd been listening to the radio, NPR, washing dishes, and heard a story. A family in rural Mississippi, location undisclosed, ran an empty commune: rows of houses stocked with clothes, heavy blankets, and sturdy shoes, and plots growing staples. "The thing is," the man who ran it said, "you can't wait until the worst happens and then start farming. You'll starve. We keep the place ready, the food ready, and provide peace of mind to the people who have a subscription. 'Course, we have more subscribers than houses, but we don't expect everyone to make it out here. We aren't in charge of that end of things." The man didn't take the sentimental view. And he and his wife and four daughters lived well.

"We don't have a plan," Lacy kept saying after she told me the story, disbelief in her voice. "We don't have a plan." As if we were the only ones.

———————

Back in the pub, all I want to do is find Lacy, walk home with her and talk, hold hands like we're girls again, because we're drunk and happy and sisters, which seems as magical as Dad ever wanted it to be, because it's brought us here. I scan the bar. The mosh-pit of dancers has dwindled to a few couples, tangled in each other and swaying to the music. I go to the bathroom and look under the stall. No Lacy.

I go out front, into the damp cool air. I'm mad at her for not being here when I need her, wandering off, exactly like her. A woman leans against a man by the door, pressing him into the wall. They each smoke a cigarette; it seems impossible that they won't burn each other.

"Have you seen an American girl? A girl with a long braid and a skirt?" They shake their heads. I walk around the pub to where Patrick is still sitting on the wall. "I can't find Lacy," I say. I sound panicky, even to myself.

"She's fine," he says. "She was with Leo."

"When?"

He looks at me and shrugs *don't worry*, then pats the wall next to him. "Come on over here." I don't move.

"She's a big girl. She's fine." I shake my head, a tremor that doesn't stop. "Andrea. You're freaking out about nothing."

"I'm not freaking out," I say, but my thoughts fly forward. She isn't a big girl. Neither am I. We are little girls, but I am that much bigger, that crucial bit. I say something to Patrick, like, *it's fine*, or *don't worry*. He nods and does look worried, but not about Lacy. I can see him reassessing me, his posture straightening, his hands no longer beckoning, and I want to assure him, to make some kind of promise, but the only words I can summon are, "I should have taken her home. She asked to go home."

I leave him, running back around to the road, which disappears into the fields in both directions, west toward the hostel, east toward the harbor. There is no reason she would have gone toward the harbor. She must have gone back to the hostel. My thinking stumbles forward like my feet in the dark, clumsy but inexorable. Past the pool of light around the pub, it's dark. Real, thick dark, the kind that cities keep at bay. After a while, my eyes adjust to the way the moon is making the puddles in the road glow. My feet are wet again.

"Lacy?" I say, intending to call out, in case she's somewhere I can't see her: lying in a ditch by the road, fallen from a boulder, strangled in a field. I hate the vivid violence that is always on the edge of my imagination. My voice comes out as a whisper, as if I'm afraid I'll call something out of the darkness.

The noise from the pub fades away like its lights. I hear crickets and wind and the waves and that's all. The half mile back home seems much longer than it did during the day. When I finally see the hostel, someone is sitting outside and I am sure that it's Lacy. I start to run.

"Hello," the person says. It's Reba.

"Is Lacy here?" I say, and she nods. "She okay?"

Reba nods again. I am so relieved that for a moment I'm not even angry.

"She had a bit too much to drink," Reba says.

I am about to go inside, but Reba stops me. "She's asleep. You let her rest. Get a glass of water and sit out here with me. I don't sleep like I used to. I need the company."

I want to go into our room and shake Lacy awake and yell at her for leaving me and hug her until I've squeezed the last thirty minutes out of us both. I want to check that she isn't sleeping on her back, suffocating on her own vomit. But Reba isn't even looking at me anymore, like she knows I'll do what she says. When I come back out with a large cup of water, she's still looking up at the sky.

"Drink that all up," she says. "Then you can have another glass. Water is the key. You don't want to be hungover when you girls go to Dun Aengus in the morning."

"I'm not drunk," I say, and it feels true. I've scared the drunk out of myself.

"I remember the first time I went to Dun Aengus. You know what it looks like? Like three stone horseshoes, one inside the other, each bigger than the next, against that cliff."

I've seen pictures. I know the cliffs are three hundred feet high. That building on the fort started in 1200 BC. That parts of it tumble into the sea as the cliffs erode.

"When I went there, there wasn't any of this tourist stuff you see now. The museum. A gift shop, for Christ's sake." She shakes her head. "But once you are past all that, it's the same as ever. No fence. Climb anything you want. But the stones are slick."

"Do people fall off?" I ask.

She looks at me like it's an odd question.

"I don't think so," she says.

I finish my glass of water.

"Why did you leave the island the first time?" I ask. "After you'd stayed that long."

There's no pause before she responds, like it's a question to which she's long ago formulated an answer. "I suppose after a year the romance had worn off a little. It was hard work, being here. And you know what they say," she flutters her hand until it lands on her leg, like a moth, "no matter where you go, there you are." She laughs to herself, as if it's a joke. "You know?"

I don't know. At least I choose not to. I am still holding out hope. Maybe if I stay here with Patrick and Leo I *will* be different, a new self to replace this old one.

I'm going to get changed, I used to say, hurrying to my room on those rare occasions Dad came home and announced we were going out for dinner.

We were hoping you'd change. An old joke, it always made him laugh.

"Patrick wants me to stay here and work," I say. I don't mention that he may have changed his mind. That if he hasn't, and I say yes, we will no doubt spend the summer having sex, because how could I not if I took the job? I think of him on the wall, holding my face in his hands, how his palms were warm and his spit sweet. I think of him staring at me, that expression of worry and confusion, the expression I hate. Now that I am calmer and the dark is only the dark again, I am embarrassed. Now that he has seen me that way, I don't want to see him again. I am in my head again, that's all. I try to shake free. Why do I always imagine falling? "I should probably finish the trip with Lacy," I say. "I should probably go home and find a real job."

"She's not a baby," Reba says, and she means it nicely,

but it sounds like what Lacy would say and I imagine that they've been talking about me.

"I know she's not a baby," I snap, my anger at Lacy flashing to Reba. You don't have to be a baby to need someone, I want to say, but that sounds childish, or like a bad song. Still, I am Lacy's someone, and she is mine, like muscle and bone. Tendons, I suddenly remember. Tendons connect muscle to bone. "It isn't qi at all," I say. My thoughts are disconnected, like an armful of balloons. Reba makes me promise I'll have another glass of water.

Back in our room, I turn Lacy from her stomach onto her side and pull a strand of hair out of her mouth. I listen to her breathe. I want to wake her up, but I don't. I imagine Reba's long fingers taking out my sister's braid, brushing her hair, and rebraiding it, like our mother used to do. Except Mom always pulled our braids too tight, like she was expecting us to encounter a tornado, like she knew it would be two days before she'd have time to braid our hair again. Eventually, I was good enough to braid our hair myself. But by then we were too old for braids.

In the morning, Lacy is already gone when I wake up. Her pack leans against the bed, strapped and ready, the bed is stripped. I had imagined waking her softly, the opposite of yesterday, respectful of our hangovers, maybe even convincing Leo to let me bring cups of coffee into the dorm. She would sit up in bed but keep her legs under the covers. She would rub her eyes, grateful for the coffee, and I would sit cross-legged at the foot of the bed and tell her all about Patrick and we would decide what I should do. She would help me make a plan. Now things are happening too fast. Now it is as if she already knows; she is showing me what it will be like when she is gone. As I strip my own sheets, I listen to the quiet, telling myself it is filled with bird songs and frogs and distant moos, not quiet at all.

In the breakfast room, Reba and Lacy sit together, and when I sit down the conversation stalls. I should talk to her now, but I can't with Reba there. Lacy tells me that her hangover isn't too bad because she threw most of it up in the pub bathroom. I envy her weak stomach. Mine, as always, has held on to everything.

And then we are at the checkout desk, packs on our backs. Everyone says it's important to get to Dun Aengus early, before there are too many people, before it looks like just another place. Patrick leans against the counter. I wonder if he even remembers the offer, or my panic. He doesn't say anything, but then he is hungover too. His slender forearm rests on the desk. Lacy hitches her pack higher on her hip. The air is damp and cool, and early sunlight begins to wash out the pale green glow of the tall corner lamp. I am here, I tell myself experimentally, and I don't ever have to go home. The moment is mine and I watch it. I am almost sure that if I ask to stay, put my hand out to touch him, he'll say yes. All I have to do is open my mouth. Instead I watch myself do nothing. Instead I think, this place will fade away the moment we are gone. It's fading away already. We are already gone.

"You girls enjoy Dun Aengus," he says.

Reba gives me a hug and then Lacy, who tears up and they both laugh. Outside, it's drizzling like it never stopped.

At the tourist kiosk we take a map. It's like Reba said. A gift shop sells wool sweaters and behind it is a little café with tea and scones and sandwiches. These buildings huddle close against the rain. Even though it's early, tourists file up the hillside like ants.

The hike to Dun Aengus is steep and we walk in silence, both breathing hard.

"What happened last night?" Lacy asks. We walk a little farther. "Reba says Patrick asked you to work here maybe." I stay silent, but though she picks up the pace in irritation, it's clear she's ready to wait me out.

"What would I do out here for a whole summer, anyway?" I finally say. "Play Scrabble?"

She turns to me, her hand on her hip, sweat on her forehead, or maybe rain.

"You'd do whatever," she says. "Whatever people do."

"What do people do?" I ask, and she smiles, like I'm making a joke, and I want to say, really though, please tell me. What might I do here? Or, what might I have done. As if living is a thing one might spontaneously do, the whole world our fucking oyster, as likely as not to clamp shut and take an arm the moment you think you're grabbing something good.

"I'm afraid," I say. I'm afraid I've ruined our trip or something deeper that should be unbreakable but isn't.

Dun Aengus is even bigger than I'd imagined. The stones are dark gray and when wet they're almost black. We walk through a door in the outer wall. The rocks are slippery, like Reba said. We walk through the second ring.

At the cliff, a few tourists peer over the edge, unconcerned. Lacy walks toward them and I go as far as I can, stopping five feet away. She walks right up to the edge and looks out, not down. In front of us is the coast of Ireland, the Cliffs of Mohr.

I imagine her slipping and falling, her arms and legs slapping the water the below.

I imagine her head cracking open like a watermelon against a rock on the way down.

I imagine her jumping, which I know is crazy, but maybe she would, without even meaning to, like I worry I may.

She looks down, then at the other people around her, calm, normal people, then back at me.

"Don't," I say. I wave at the sky in front of her. "Just, don't."

Lacy takes one last glance down, then walks back to me.

"I'll tell you what we'll do," she says, sounding like the big sister. She takes my hand, her fingers curling around mine as if we are ready to cross the street. We take a few steps forward together, until we can begin to see over the edge to the water below. Then she kneels, pulling me down with her. The wet grass soaks through the knees of my jeans.

"Alright," she says, and she draws her lower lip in between her teeth, like she's done for as long as I can remember. She lies down on the grass and I lie beside her. We crawl forward, like soldiers, heads down, until our eyes, noses, lips come over the edge. Below us, a seagull is flying over the water, watching for the splash of a fish. And I feel, even though we are on solid ground, that the cliff may crumble and pitch us into the air, our fingers still entwined.

MARCY BREAKS UP
WITH HERSELF

There's this one show I'm obsessed with right now called *20 Below*. The hosts are a Canadian couple, Anette and Steve, who go to people's houses and the wife Anette throws out most of their stuff and the husband Steve talks to them about how it's okay to love themselves and hate their fathers. The stuff that gets thrown out goes to Goodwill or the dump, you don't see that part, and you don't see the fathers either, but the mothers are usually there, often crying, saying how grateful they are. By the end of the episode, the person has only twenty "nonessential" items (*20 Below* referring to this ideal number and to how cold it gets, I guess, in northern Canada) and they are so happy. *I feel like a new person*, they say. And I think, I would be *amazing* as a new person. I ask my boyfriend, Josh, to nominate me, but he won't. He says I already spend too much time at home watching television.

"Exactly," I say. "If I was on the show, I wouldn't do that anymore."

Josh pauses like he wants to say something he's probably said before, about how I need to be more proactive, how I am too preoccupied with the little things, how it's creepy that when I have a bruise I poke it because it feels good, or whatever you call good when it's painful.

"I'm not letting the Canadians throw away our television," he says finally, and takes his dish to the sink and scrapes spaghetti into the disposal. Even though I'm full—especially because I'm full—I think about the bag of chips in the pantry and I want to eat them all in one sitting but I tell myself *no*, I tell myself, *I know! I'll* write a letter to the network and I'll get Janice to sign it, since Janice is up for just about anything. *Marcy has enormous potential*, I imagine writing. *With a little help, Marcy could be a different person. Marcy would be better as a different person. Marcy is incapable without your help of becoming a different person. Would it be worth it to make Marcy a different person?* I decide maybe I won't write that letter after all.

I get up and wash my dish and shout at Josh, who is in the other room, that I took the garbage out while he was at work, and I'm glad that he's put his earbuds in, glad that he can't hear about what passes for an accomplishment some days.

When Josh moves out a week later, he takes the TV, the gaming console, his clothes, most of the towels, and the scented oil diffuser that I'd gotten him as a gift and only I ever used. I call my friend Janice and tell her that the oil diffuser is gone and now the apartment smells like it used to, like there's a damp spot moldering somewhere.

"I can't find it," I say as I get to my knees and stretch my hand out, patting under the couch, finding only dry carpet, crumbs, a crochet hook.

"I can come over, babe," she says. "If you're upset."

I sit back on my heels, feel that stretch in my arches, another good kind of pain. "Maybe I'm looking at this all wrong," I say.

"I can come over when I get off tonight," she says. Janice and I are cocktail waitresses at Pan's Palace, a fancy name for a place where we wear high-waisted short shorts and tight tops. I worked last night, serving drinks, followed by having drinks at the kind of shit bar that exists for servers to blow off steam. I passed out on the couch; it wasn't until I woke up that I saw the TV was gone.

"Maybe this is a sign," I say, looking at the dust-free circle left by the diffuser. "One less nonessential thing."

Janice isn't much for signs. "You call me if you need me," she says, and hangs up.

I take the note Josh left, some bullshit about wanting to avoid a scene but he'll call me later, soon, he promises, and I put it in the garbage disposal, grinding it to pulp, pouring the gallon of skim milk in after it, the kind of milk *he* likes, horrible, thin, tinted blue like the skin over a vein.

The one-bedroom apartment feels empty without Josh but also lighter, room in the closet where the towels were, room on the coffee table where the television was, room in my chest now that the bad thing I knew would happen has happened. I make a piece of cinnamon sugar toast and microwave some old coffee. Without the non-essential TV, I start an episode of *20 Below* on my laptop. This episode, a woman who owns a two-bedroom house in Quebec has been nominated by her sister. Even though this woman is a successful veterinarian, her home is a "filthy mess," "dark pit," and "constant source of despair for the rest of the family" (so says the judgmental sister). Anette and Steve are on the job.

There are two parts of the show that I love best. One is when they first get to the house or apartment and the person who lives there has to show them each room.

This is when you find out how ready the subject is to go through this process, how eager they are for help, how bad they've let things get. The veterinarian is embarrassed as she shows Anette the bedroom, but she tries to play it off with humor. The closet is empty, hangers clacking, because clothes are piled on two chairs: the dirty chair and the clean chair. "At least there's a system," the woman says with a strained laugh and Anette smiles, tight-lipped.

"These are kitchen chairs," Anette says. Anette has very dark hair that frames her pale face with very straight bangs. She always carries a clipboard. In the veterinarian's living room, a small saucepan is being used as a candle holder. Wax fills the pot halfway. I love it. Anette does not. Anette gives the veterinarian her version of a compliment: "You are disorganized and chaotic. But you are not dirty." I crunch through my cinnamon toast. I shake my head gently. They have a lot of work ahead of them to get down to twenty items.

"I don't think I can do it," the veterinarian says. "I don't think it's reasonable."

"Imagine," Anette says, "that you are a hunter-gatherer and you can only keep what you can carry your back."

The veterinarian nods but, though I love the show, I find this particular argument unconvincing. I am not a hunter-gatherer. I would die as a hunter-gatherer.

Yes, Anette says, *you would. But at least you'd lose some of that weight first.*

Steve is talking to the veterinarian about her relationship with her sister when my mother calls to see how I'm doing.

"How are you doing?" she says.

"I'm fine," I say. "I'm thinking of getting rid of a bunch of my shit."

"I saw a documentary about how Goodwill throws out ninety percent of donations."

"I don't think that's true," I say. It might be true. But I'm not trying to pick a fight. "If you could only keep like twenty things, what do you think you would keep?"

"My passport," she says.

"But like, nonessential things."

"Your father."

My mother thinks she's very funny so, as a punishment for her and a treat to myself, I don't tell her that Josh has left me.

When I hang up, with the show still paused, the apartment is very quiet. The damp spot is starting to itch me from the inside. I can smell it. I check the corners of the room and under the couch again. *Fine fine fine*, I hum to myself. *Everything is fine fine fine.* The chips are in the pantry but I won't eat them. The damp spot is all in my head.

(I know that smell is coming from somewhere. I just have to find it.)

I put on an apron and a pink bandana and get a box of trash bags, the thick black ones strong enough to hide liquor bottles and bodies. I start in the kitchen because that is where Anette and Steve always start. Not many sentimental items in the kitchen. Besides, Anette isn't a monster. A lot in a kitchen *is* essential. A small frying pan, a large frying pan, and a large pot: essential. Six plates, bowls, spoons, forks, knives: essential. The juicer: nonessential. I put it in a cardboard box on which I've written SHIT WEIGHING YOU DOWN!!!! in Sharpie, which everyone knows is the pen you use when you mean business. The juicer is technically Josh's, so that one feels good. Two nonessential pans follow. My mother got me an Instapot for Christmas because she said I should learn to cook, except Instapots aren't about learning to cook. They are about learning how to take shortcuts to avoid learning how to cook, which is why I am the perfect person to own an Instapot. Steve is not a fan of shortcuts. I put it in the box.

By the time I'm done in the kitchen, there is only one

nonessential thing I've kept. It's a mug, white with a blue drawing of a duck. The duck has completely round eyes, like it's terrified or high, and on the side of the mug it says Le Canard, which I have always assumed but never confirmed is French for duck. I found it in a thrift store while I was in college and I remember realizing that I could simply buy it, that I didn't need to drink out of mugs I'd stolen from the dining hall. I'd taken it home and set it lovingly on the shelf over my desk, twisting it so that the duck had its round eyes on me. I take the mug now into the living room and put it on the empty shelf I've designated for my twenty items.

"One," I say.

In the kitchen, I pick up the box and the bottom of it splits because really, what was I thinking putting that much in the box when I have these trash bags? A wineglass shatters on the kitchen tile and I stand still for a moment, an island surrounded by an ocean of glass, sure I'll cut myself, wishing there was someone to hear me call for help.

how u doin babe still okay?

Janice is a very good friend.

soooo good! I reply. cleaned out kitchen going to tackle bedroom. stopped looking for damp spot!!

That last one is a bit of a lie. Janice texts me back a face with its brain exploding out the top. Janice knows when I'm full of shit. Then she says, c u at work tmr and I push that right out of my mind, it's an eternity before I have to go to work, and besides, by then I'll probably be someone who enjoys her job.

No, actually, I'll never enjoy working at Pan's Palace.

I admit, I lose a bit of steam in the bedroom. Bedrooms are harder. I know what Anette would say. She'd tell me that pushing through this feeling shows I'm serious about the process. Steve would say that I deserve to be loved despite my imperfections, which isn't as helpful, but I'll take it. I imperfectly stuff a bunch of clothes into a trash bag. A little black dress that hasn't fit in a few years. A T-shirt that rides up too high, exposing the tops of my hips. A jaunty cap that has never looked good on me, not even in the store, but I bought it anyway and I didn't know why I was doing it even then. A gray turtleneck that makes my tits look enormous, *but at least it hides your stomach.* That is exactly the kind of shit I need to get rid of. I pull the ties on the trash bag so hard that one tears off.

Anette looks at me with disapproval. *This is a meditative process*, she says. *Stop being such a fucking spaz.*

I look into my closet for more to get rid of. Anette says that essential clothing has to be defined by the individual. A businesswoman will need different shoes than a nurse. My waitressing shoes are black sneakers with thick tread and thick soles and still my feet always ache at the end of the night. I put them in a corner with my uniform: two pairs of black shorts, two pairs of ankle-high black socks, three tight white t-shirts with the Pan's Palace logo splashed large across the front. I always scrub baking soda into the armpits before I wash them to try to get out the stains.

The other categories of essential clothing that Anette recognizes are sleepwear, formal wear, and casual. I put a sports bra, tank top, and set of boy shorts next to my uniform for sleepwear.

I know what to do next. I've seen Anette do it many times. Remove each item one by one, try it on, decide if it really fits, admit if you haven't worn it in a year. I hold up a dress I like, blue with small white flowers, a scoop neck and flouncy hem, and I decide I am not quite ready for this. I don't want to know if it doesn't fit, suddenly I know it *won't* fit, there's that itchy feeling back again, and I put the dress back because I'll definitely deal with this later. And it isn't like I should be throwing clothes away willy nilly. Unlike that veterinarian, I'm not made of money.

Even though my bedroom is by no means stripped down to essentials, I add three more items to my nonessential shelf. First, a blue vase my college boyfriend made me in a ceramics class, the glaze done to look like the vase had been broken and then glued back together. My stuffed animal Heather the narwhal, who, with Josh gone, will sleep under my arm again. A heavy iron bottle opener in the shape of a mermaid that I stole from a vintage shop downtown. Josh once asked me where I got it and I made up a lie and then hid it in my underwear drawer.

There's a full-length mirror in the living room. It was Josh's and I'm surprised he left it. He liked to look at himself before he went to work. Once, when we were high, he made me sit in front of it with him even though he knew I hate to look at myself in the mirror.

"Sometimes," he said, "it's like I am not sure I exist. It's like I need to see myself in the mirror to be sure I'm still here."

I turn the mirror to face the wall. When I'm a new person, looking at myself in the mirror is exactly the kind of thing I'll like to do.

By midnight, I've filled a lot of trash bags. I'm exhausted and nowhere near having only twenty nonessential items.

How does anyone do this when they have to go through a whole house? I turn on another episode of the show. Obviously, I've seen all of them already, but that's not the point. Besides, I notice new things every time. I said before I love two things about *20 Below*? The second is what happens at the very end of each episode, after the veterinarian—or chef or teacher or urban planner—has discovered how much happier they are to be a new person. In the final two minutes or so of the show, either Anette or Steve reveals one of their twenty below. This episode, it's Anette's turn.

When it comes to her twenty, Anette is pretty pragmatic. She has a whittling set (which is a bunch of small things, but in one box, so it's okay). A pair of jade earrings that were her mom's. A fishing pole. And my favorite thing of hers so far, a plastic Mickey Mouse that fits in the palm of her hand. Its ears have been rubbed so many times the black has worn off, revealing the flesh-colored plastic beneath. Anette is not one to make a fuss, but you can see on her face when she holds it, she loves it, and so I love it too.

Only three seasons of *20 Below* have come out, six episodes each, which means they've shared eighteen of the forty total nonessential items. It's very exciting. I used to talk to Josh about it, speculating about what the other twenty-two items might be and worrying that the show would be canceled before we saw them all.

"You know it's probably bullshit, right?" Josh said. "Those people are making all this money from this show. There's no way they actually only have like two space heaters and a cupcake tin."

I told him he didn't know anything at all about anything and left the room.

There are many signs that a relationship will not work out. This was one of them.

Though I'm planning to get up early and keep working, I sleep late and barely have time to stuff my car full of trash bags before I drive to lunch with my mother. We meet at a fish taco place and on the wall is a painting of a smiling fish nestled in a tortilla.

"Do you think that fish knows he's about to be eaten alive?" I ask my mother.

"Do we have to talk about that every time we eat here?" she says. We each bite our tacos, cabbage and white sauce falling out the ends.

Mom has never been one to fill a silence. It's her superpower, and so I blurt out, "Josh broke up with me," even though I'd planned to roll it out at the very end of the meal when she'd have no time to comment. I always do this. Speak before I want to, admit what I don't want to.

"Oh Marcy," she says, and I hear it exactly the way she means it.

"He was beating me," I say.

"No he wasn't."

"It wasn't working. He liked cooking shows and said he didn't understand why anyone would want to get a tattoo."

Mom shakes her head and takes another bite of taco.

"He didn't like that I slept in so much. But you have to when you wait tables."

"I actually had something I wanted to discuss with you today," she says, after dabbing the corners of her mouth with a clean napkin. My napkin is in a shredded, sticky ball. "Your father and I are selling the house."

"The house?" I say. "My house?"

"Our house. The house you haven't lived in in years. We put it on the market a while ago and now we have a buyer. We're selling it and moving to Las Cruces. Your father wants to start painting."

"You love that house," I say.

"It's a house." Mom sighs. "Dear." She takes my hand. "Your father and I are ready for a change." I imagine

Anette and Steve rubbing their hands together, the entire house disappearing until there is nothing but black garbage bags. "We knew you'd be upset," she says.

"I'm not upset about the house. I'm upset about *Josh*," I say. I tell her I can't believe how incredibly unsupportive she's being right now.

Mom tells me we'll talk about this again soon because she needs me to clean my boxes out of the garage. "Maybe you and your brothers can get a storage unit together."

"I'm decluttering my life!" I'm being too loud. The fish on the wall is meeting his death with a lot more dignity than I'm displaying. "And I'm throwing away the Instapot."

"You should at least offer it to Josh first," she says.

I hope she knows that sometimes she's a bitch.

I'd expected to feel happy as I dropped my bags off at the Goodwill, but lunch has ruined my moment of triumph. I carry one of the bags in the front door and an elderly employee tells me no, donations go around the back, and when I take my car around I see a pile of things by a locked metal door. Most people who donate aren't as organized as me. There's a doll lying inside a lamp shade. An open plastic tub filled with VHS tapes.

A toaster oven still full of crumbs. I lean my bags against the wall. I'm sweating when I'm finally done unloading everything. In my purse, my phone chimes.

> *sorry i had to end things that way. i hope you know i care about you*

I don't text him back.

my mom is selling our house so they can move to las cruces, I text Janice.

las cruces is dope, she says.

Janice doesn't get it. I don't know if I get it. The house was a cramped place for three kids and it's too big for just my parents. The upstairs hall was narrow and dark and the stairs were covered in a red-orange carpet that came off on my socks and burned my knees when I tripped. The backyard was nice but my dad was always ripping it up to try a new kind of grass, and the grass always died. In Las Cruces, they'll have a rock garden and plant a cactus or two. When I come to visit, maybe we'll eat dinner outside. Deserts get cold quickly when the sun sets. In fact, that's exactly what my dad will say.

"Can't believe how quickly it gets cold when the sun's down!"

And we'll nod and say, yes, how amazing.

"It's so great when you have time to visit," Mom will say.

And it will be great, because by then I'll be a different person.

It's 2:00 when I get home. I should be at work by 5:00. I open a beer and don't drink it. I pour a glass of water on the carpet to make a wet spot and I rub it hard over and over with a towel until I soak up every drop, until you can barely tell it's there. I smell it and it smells like damp carpet. Nothing sinister. Somehow, the apartment doesn't look noticeably more empty, even after all that work. I am going to do a little more cleaning, straighten things up, and instead I lie down on the couch and open my laptop and take a sip of that beer after all. I look up *20 Below* on YouTube and find a new interview, or at least one I haven't seen before. It's just Steve, which is unusual. Anette is the forceful personality. She's the one who gets things done, who people make into memes. Anette holding a dustpan full of dog hair saying THIS IS YOUR LIFE. Anette opening a closet and being hit in the head with a soccer ball. Sometimes I think Steve is there because Anette doesn't know what to do with people once she's made them cry.

In this interview, Steve is in his blue plaid shirt and

jeans. You get to know their outfits really well, because they don't have many, and this is one of my favorites because it brings out his eyes. It's some Canadian show and the woman interviewing him looks high school young. She asks Steve what advice he has for young people who are just starting out, who are making "home spaces" for the first time.

"That's a great question," Steve says. He'd say that no matter what. "As we get older, items we purchase begin to have less meaning. They're functional rather than sentimental. I'd say, as a young person just starting out, buy only what you really, really plan to keep. Would you be willing to move with it? Because you'll have to. Again and again. But I'll also say, if you do own something you love, that you can tell a story about, don't let anyone tell you to get rid of it or tell you it's trash. Hold on to it."

The girl nods, her face serious, and doesn't ask the obvious follow up question. *What has Anette made you give away that you regret?*

It's 4:30 which means I'm already late. My head feels heavy in that way I recognize. It would be so easy to lie on my bed and call in sick. Lie on the bed and not make the call at all. I would be too embarrassed to stay home if I knew Josh was getting off work in an hour. I would know that if I did crawl under the covers, Josh would come sit beside me on the bed and stroke my hair and ask if I was feeling okay.

Okay, no. No, no, no. Fucking Steve is in my head, sensitive Steve who I imagine oiling his little league glove one last time before donating it to some sick kid. Steve and the action figure he kept in its box for as long as he could stand before he got it out and played with it, before Anette made him give it to an orphan. Steve is no help. I need Anette.

You really do, she says.

My uniform is still on the floor of the bedroom and I pick it up, strip to my underwear. I always feel a twinge of anxiety before I put on the shorts and shirt. The uniform is intentionally "form fitting," says my manager. "Slutty," says Janice.

You know you're on the verge, Anette says.

I pull the shorts on and button and zip. Are they tighter than usual? They feel too tight.

You've probably gained weight, Anette says.

I haven't, though. I wore these forty-eight hours ago. Nothing changes that fast.

Forty-eight hours ago you had a boyfriend and your parents still owned their house.

The button is digging into my stomach. It itches, I

swear, it feels all wrong. My stomach rises a little over the waist band. Does it always? I rip them off and try on the other pair and I think it's worse, like they both shrunk in the dryer. I don't remember putting them in the dryer. I walk to the kitchen to get scissors, still in my underwear, the blinds open, but I don't care, and I pick up the shorts and carve into them, cut each leg of the short from top to bottom and I do the same to the other pair. It takes force. The denim is thick and tough. Then I cut the shirts into scraps. I even cut the little ankle socks up. I almost stab the black shoes, but then I think about how they protect me, or at least they try. I put them back in the corner.

I pull armfuls of clothes from the closet. I cut the sleeves off a plain black shirt. Nothing wrong with it but nothing right either. I cut up T-shirts and running shorts and a sweatshirt that's a little tight in the shoulders and a sweatshirt that has always fit perfectly. I cut through the closet until there is nothing left but the blue dress with the little white flowers and even though Steve would tell me not to, I cut the dress in half and one side crumples to the floor. The side still in my hand hangs limp, somehow more human now. What was I afraid of? I drop it to the floor too.

I cut off the underwear I'm in. I cut the clasp between the cups of my bra. This is good. I'm naked. I wait for the itching feeling to stop. Maybe I should burn my clothes. But burning is harder than it seems. People die in fires, cities are laid waste, and yet so little is as flammable as you hope. No way to donate them now and it's better this way. No effort should be taken to preserve, to save them from the dump and dirt and rain and rot. It seems wrong in the middle of this mess that my skin remains unmarked. It seems wrong to leave so much of what is still wrong with me there, out in the open, when I could carve myself away, carve myself into something truly good and new.

I put the scissors on the bed and walk back to the living room. My phone is on the table. I have a text from Janice. where r u???? I turn off my phone.

You know what's holding you back? Anette asks. I pick up the vase with the beautiful cracked glaze and drop it to the ground. I expect it to shatter, but it doesn't. It breaks into three pieces and I pick up the smallest piece, a triangle with two sharp edges, the third edge the lip of the vase. I use it to cut open the bag of chips in the cupboard and then I bring both with me to sit in front of the full length mirror, which I turn back around.

There is something about ugliness that demands more ugliness. Why be a girl with an average face when I can be a wolfman? A creature from the black lagoon? I eat a chip. I force myself to look, to see the heavy weight of my tits, the way they don't sag exactly, not yet, but they will. And my waist which is okay at that certain angle when I suck in a bit and arch my back and I'm doing that, arching and squirming. I let out a deep sigh, relax muscles that do not want to relax. My stomach rounds. My thighs are dimpled. I eat another chip and don't even feel bad because I know I'm going to eat the whole bag; it was decided the moment I opened it. I look at my strange pussy with ruffled labia like a bed duster. I look at my elegant neck and strong arms and calloused feet and wide nipples. My mother's nose and my father's chin and my brown-green-muddled eyes that refuse to blink because if I look away for a moment I'll look away for another month or year or lifetime. Instead I eat another chip, swipe the grease off my fingers and onto the carpet next to me. The carpet is wet next to me.

Is this the wet spot I made or the one I've been looking for?

I lie on the floor, the shard in my hand, looking at the shelf that now has only three nonessential items, nothing at all really. I could add some photos, I think. Or the letter my little brothers sent me when I was at camp that my mom laminated for me, so strange, so unlike her. I wonder what is in those boxes at home in the garage, if some essential part of me is buried there. Because I realize that it's the twenty items that are essential, not the rest of it, not the pans I can replace or the oil diffuser that Josh will never use, that will force him to remember me until he finally gives it away.

I press the edge of the shard against my stomach and realize I have no idea how hard to press. What would be enough? What would hurt in exactly that right way, enough to distract, never enough to be seen.

Are you going to just lie there? Anette asks, and I don't know what she's asking. If she means get on with it. If she means get up. I can't let her watch me doing this. She wouldn't understand. I wish Steve were here, I think, but that's not right either. I set the shard down. Maybe I can glue the vase back together. The best thing about it was that it already looked broken.

Janice arrives around midnight. She has a key and lets herself in.

"You should still be at work," I say.

"It was slow tonight. I took first cut."

Janice never takes first cut. She needs the money. We all do.

Janice stands still for a moment and then puts down her purse and takes the bottle of wine to the kitchen. It's a screw top, which is good. "Where the fuck are the wineglasses?" I hear her say, and she comes back instead with two cereal bowls. She pours some wine into each bowl and sets them down next to me. Then she takes off all of her clothes. She looks right at me as she does it. Janice has dimples on her thighs too. Her waist is thin and her breasts are small and on the right one is a red-brown splash that must be a birthmark. She sits down next to me. I get up on my elbows and try to drink the wine but the angle is strange and I choke on it. Wine runs down my chin and over my breasts into my belly button and she leans over and licks a drop off my neck.

Janice grins. She takes a drink herself and doesn't spill a drop. She takes the shard from my side and throws it across the room. She stares at me. I worry she's in the wet spot but I don't ask. I don't ask if I'm fired. I don't ask if she can see what I've done, what an incredible mess I've made. I don't want to ever speak again. I want her to keep looking at me exactly like this: calm and wild and like she sees exactly who I am, every hidden place. I want her look at me, to be my eyes, and to never, never stop.

THE BEST AND ONLY WHORE OF CWM HYFRYD, PATAGONIA, 1886

I have sex with the men of Cwm Hyfryd so their wives don't have to. Wives, for the most part, are grateful; this is a hard place for new life. The town is barely that, a collection of cabins spread apart by miles, no general store or midwife. The men are grateful too; I never tell their secrets. Ask anyone if I can be trusted. If a man enjoys my company and some other man wants to know what we did, I'll say, that man? That man standing over there? He was up fast as a boy, swived me bowlegged, and smacked my ass when it was over. Tipped me extra he'd put himself in such a good humor, came back a week later to say I'd cured his gout. It makes every man smile to hear it, happy to imagine that if he visits me, the same will be said of him.

When a man comes to the door of my cabin, he brings a bag of meal or a bit of dried beef; sometimes, if I am lucky, a bottle of moonshine to pull from or a bit of sugar for baking. Money is less use here, though I take it when it is offered. Money is always worth having. When we have sex it is each to his taste, though I do not tolerate being slapped around or handled too roughly and it is easier here than in Wales to make sure of it. Women, whores in particular, are less disposable when we are scarce. I am willing to suck a man's prick if I know he's a good man, if I consider him a friend, because a good man will be grateful but a bad one will think a prick suck means he owns you. I sometimes enjoy the sex—these men aren't strangers anymore—but often I simply tolerate it. It never hurts to have had a bit of moonshine first.

Whether we have sex or not, the evening usually ends with the man napping in front of my fire. I like to watch them sleep and wonder if they dream of home. When they wake, I do not inquire, because I would not answer the same question, if anyone thought to ask me.

All men are different, but what is true of all of the men of Cwm Hyfryd is that they are tired. In the spring, snow melt from the mountain floods our fields and sometimes our houses. The paths are so muddy they are impossible to use, worse even than in the winter. The summer is too short to let us fix what needs to be mended and the fall is over as soon as the crops are taken in, if not sooner. We grow potatoes and carrots, shoot and cure meat until our cabins are more larder than home. When I write to my brother in Wales, I say that come early November, I am as a mouse who has burrowed a hole in a block of cheese; I stay inside getting fat all winter long. He writes back to say his son now pictures all the houses of Patagonia as cubes of fine cheddar and begs to come. His son is too small to know that we will never meet, that I have come too far to go back. I also write my brother stories of my reliable husband, a strong man who enjoys pushing plows and keeping the barn stocked with wood. My brother is too good and honest a man to worry with the truth. He worries already and does not understand why I have moved from Rawson, where the rest of the Welsh settlers are, where the irrigation has made the land easier.

I write, *I left for the foothills of the Andes because I am foolish and because I do not care to go to church.* I write, *If I'd wanted to walk down a cobbled street and take afternoon tea, I could have saved myself a long journey.* There are no cobbled streets in Rawson, no afternoon tea you do not make yourself, but it is nice to think so, to imagine streets and tea so close, to imagine I am choosing to forgo such luxuries.

I write, *Do not worry. I promise I am well. This place will not last long as an outpost. People are always arriving, pushed out by the arrivals behind them. If we keep this up, we will all be back where we started.*

I love to be alone and I am never more alone than after a man leaves. All the space he occupied—the chair, the cup, the looks my way that ask what I am thinking, the glance of the hand against my body, yet another question I have to answer—suddenly, he is out the door, and that chair is mine to sit in. If I were always alone, though, I would start to glance my own way, to bother myself with foolishness. For example, sometimes, when I am chopping wood, I try to think of a word different from *whore* because whore is not a pretty word. That in itself is not bad, for I am not pretty and sex is not pretty. The natural world is not pretty either; it is nothing so weak and neither am I. Last winter, I shot a wolf. When I was ten, I began work in a cotton mill. When I was thirteen I lost my middle finger in the machine.

Really, I sometimes think, it is not the word *whore* I mind so much. But I do have other occupations. I am a farmer. I am handy with a needle and thread, despite the missing finger. I do a good job patching clothes and wounds. I can read and I own a Bible. They might call me whore if they also call me surgeon and minister and friend.

When I am happy, which is my temperament, I write to my brother and tell him what the Andes look like in the summer, not as green as the hills of home, but so high as to make me always look up to God. I tell him that the pampas are not fertile like we were promised, but that Welsh work has made them better. That it was a good Welsh woman, Rachel Jenkins, who imagined the irrigation system in Rawson, and more than that, imagined it so hard and well it came into being. Now the river Camwy floods and fertilizes on command. It makes me proud to write it and I like to think of my brother reading my letters by his fire, with his wife and his son nearby, telling them all what a woman can do. I miss him and I sign my letters *love* and hope every one will reach his door.

When I am melancholy, I write to my older sister, who is dead, and I burn the letters I write to her in my fire. She would not have liked to imagine the Andes, as my brother does. Too big. Too unlike home. She would have said, *cariad, come back to bed. We have work in the morning. Why do you always make things harder? They are hard already.*

When I was a girl, a man came through my village in northern Wales, passing out pamphlets about the new Patagonian colony. His voice was loud as he tried to attract a crowd, severe as a preacher's, promising that better place. "A new home for us," he said. "We will thrive, and not be bothered." My sister was with me, tugged at me though I dug my heels in. I wanted to watch him. There was little enough excitement.

"Do you think it's true?" I asked. Verdant, fertile fields. Hard labor rewarded with honest living. Enough for everyone.

My sister shook her head. "Whether it is or isn't, it has nothing to do with us."

I pulled my arm away from her, angry, and walked through the small gathering to take a pamphlet anyway. The man made me show I could read before he let me have it. "That is good," he said. "We need women like you." I glowed.

"You're wasting that man's paper," my sister said, to me and to him. "More than he's wasted it already."

I wonder if my sister would say the letters I write to her are a waste. No doubt she would. She had only the beginnings of cotton lung that summer, a small cough in the night, a tightness in her chest that made her sour and frightened, not like the sister I had known, who had helped me keep my hair so tidy, who had taught me the right songs to sing to make the bread rise. It would be four more years before she finished suffocating on her own breath. So many pieces of cotton inhaled, I imagine her lungs became pillows.

The air inside the mill is kept humid, so the thread will not break. Here the air is thin. I breathe deep and still want more. I want to feel how much I can take.

I could have stayed in Rawson, but I could not have stayed in Wales. There are always things we will not do to save ourselves, ways we will and will not sell our bodies. I would not watch that slow death again, or die it myself.

Patagonia is a land with more sky than earth. *I wish you could see it*, I write to brother and sister. In the pampas, the brush huddles close to the ground, afraid of the air and right to be. It punishes. Sometimes I lie on the ground with the bushes, to feel as they do, a moment away from being plucked and tumbled. I never forget that here I am rootless. I am careful to have no children and am every year less likely. It is a miracle to be this far from home, a blessing if I can remember to take it.

At least, when the men of Cwn Hyfryd come to visit me, I know exactly where I am. I am whole and warm and full of conversation. I am across the room. I am by their side. I am beneath. I am above. I am making a pot of tea just so, and pouring it into two mugs. I am in the vacant chair again, at last, and even then they ground me. I am where they recently were. I am held still in the heat of their bodies, and this way, I can live a practical life, and revel in the moments I do become untethered, when I am across and below and above, when I am plucked and tumbled, a small kite broken free. Then, I float up the Andes, fly with the condors and shout down greetings to the grazing vicuñas. *Pob lwc! Siwrne ddiogel! Good luck! Safe journey!* I fly until I am so high I have reached God's arms and He waits with me awhile, passing time in quiet until he sets me back down again, refreshed and able to continue my work.

So I am contented. And on the nights when my missing finger throbs and aches, I hold the stump tight and tell my body that the finger is gone, that all this protest will not bring it back.

MIDWESTERN GIRL IS TIRED OF APPEARING IN YOUR SHORT STORIES

Midwestern Girl goes to New York City, and she reminds the protagonist (of course she is not the protagonist) of everything he has left behind. He covets her innocence and also despises it. When she gives up and returns home, he is sad, but not surprised.

A flick of your wrist. Midwestern Girl stands alone at a house party. The protagonist smiles at her, as if to say, *cheer up* and *I notice subtle things*, and this reminds the reader that the protagonist is secretly sensitive, no matter what terrible things he has done or will do. He and Midwestern Girl never speak, and the story leaves her to sip her beer in a corner. In the living room, the protagonist punches his best friend. Will he turn out to be like his father? He ends the night hanging out with two strangers. They walk to the East River and throw rocks into the fathomless deep.

A knuckle crack. Midwestern Girl walks down the street wearing a low-cut green blouse. As the protagonist passes, he takes a moment to admire her ample breasts before returning to his main concern, *what will happen if I don't sell these exotic macaws before Ricky demands the money?* When it starts to pour, the protagonist ducks into the first doorway he sees, only to find himself in a boutique sex shop. A woman is already there—has she just come in, like him? But no. While his bangs drip into his eyes, her bland beige coat is dry. (Midwestern Girl looks down to see her low-cut top gone, her pants suddenly waist high and itchy.) *It sure is pouring*, he says, and she says, *This is nothing like the rain in Ohio.* She must be embarrassed, he thinks, to be caught sifting through a bin of purple butt plugs. *It's a gift for my niece's bachelorette party*, she says.

This is Midwestern Girl's life. She bobs for apples. She laughs guilelessly. She is appalled by the price of serve-yourself froyo (*six dollars!* she exclaims, while the New Yorkers in line behind her roll their eyes at her ignorance). She inhabits the edges of scenes and delivers remarks on the weather. She is pretty but never beautiful. She is silent but never mysterious. From time to time, standing at the edge of a crowded room as the story moves away from her, she wonders about the Midwest. She has heard herself say that she misses its squeaky cheese curds, its deep snows, its particular kind of good people. Though she is from there, she has never been.

For reasons at first obscure to Midwestern Girl, you become obsessed with road trips.

A man travels from New York to San Francisco. He stops at an antique mall, where Midwestern Girl convinces him to buy a rusty horseshoe. *Every new home needs a little luck,* she winks. He gets drunk in Las Vegas and loses it in a bet.

A man travels from New York to Florida. There's no reason for Midwestern Girl to be in this story, but there she is at a rest stop in Virginia, gas pump in her hand. *Iowa,* the man says, looking at her car's tags. *You're a long way from home.*

Am I? she wonders.

A man travels from New York to anywhere else, having left behind his wife and all her expectations. He meets Midwestern Girl in a bar by the Motel 8. He and Midwestern Girl talk over beers and she restores his faith in humanity with her innocent wit, her no-nonsense advice. He returns to his wife.

Rewind the scene. The man and Midwestern Girl talk over whiskey then walk back to her room; in the hall, they begin to kiss and she fumbles for her room key. She has been kissed before—it has been clear all night, in her bold eyes and suggestive top—yet she cannot remember it. Does a kiss always taste so half-hearted? She leans into him, traces his jaw with her finger. She knows he'll stop even before he places his hand on hers, the door just barely cracked. *You should go back to your wife*, she says, but what she wants to say is, *Do it again, but mean it.*

Rewind the scene. Midwestern Girl is the bartender, and the protagonist barely notices her (though he does spare a moment for those ample breasts). He hits on a woman from Portland who has tattoos and is damaged in a way that creates its own gravity. They go out into the parking lot and throw empty bottles at the stars. Midwestern Girl wipes the bar in a wide circle, over and over and over. She has been almost content to sit at the edge of these stories, but she remembers all the dialogue she's spoken in this motel bar, the kiss she's taken, and she resents that Portland Woman will be kissed with enthusiasm and abandon. She wants to go outside and not only to watch them. She wants to see where she is, someplace more specific than between one spot and the next.

The protagonist and Portland Woman come back in and he leaves his wedding ring in the tip jar. Rewind the scene. The protagonist comes back in alone.

Surprised you're still open, he says to Midwestern Girl. *They're working you too hard.*

I'm tired, she says, and she means it.

A man travels from New York to Reno and sees Midwestern Girl hitchhiking west of Omaha. (Her heart soars! What a thing for her to do! The gravel on the side of the road bruises her feet. Why is she wearing flip flops when she has hiking boots tied to the outside of her oversized pack?) The man pulls over to the side of the two-lane highway and picks her up. (Should she be getting into this car? Her feet insist she will, though she tries to hold them to the hot asphalt.) Once she is buckled in, the car speeding down the road, the man tells her she shouldn't hitchhike. Doesn't she know it's dangerous, especially for a beautiful girl like her? (Is this his way of saying *he* is a danger, or just the entire rest of the world?) She smiles coyly, and says, *good thing I met you, then*. They pass through Lincoln, Kearney, Cozad, North Platte, Ogallala—though the man has driven through this country before, this time he sees it through her eyes, which are so bright and hopeful. She becomes less anxious as the hours pass, though she is always aware of him, and for once, as she looks out the window, her look of innocent excitement is not a mask. She has never traveled before, never seen so many miles in every direction. Their conversation is dull. *It's a beautiful day outside*, she says, but it isn't what she wants to say. She wants to say that she enjoys rain as much as sunshine, that she loves when snow obliterates the features of a landscape. She wants to shout her desire for a storm that will pluck trees from the ground like daisies. When the Rockies finally come into view, her breath catches in a tiny hitch. *The plains*, she says, *the plains are gone so suddenly*, and for the first time, Midwestern Girl feels the joy of thought and speech colliding, and *you* feel the singe of her pleasure in your fingertips. You want, for a moment, to linger with her. But she is only a small part of the story. The man lets her off in Boulder and watches her in the rearview mirror to see if she'll turn around. She doesn't. As she walks, she thinks, maybe I can get lost here. But with a snap, she's gone.

A father and son are on their way to a funeral and stop in Nebraska for gas. Midwestern Girl serves them their coffee and they sit at the diner bar to sip it, warming their hands around the mugs. She has ample breasts, yes, but these are pillows, comforting, a place to rest. She says "oh gee" in an accent no Nebraskan has ever used, but that doesn't matter for the story. The accent is there to make a point. There are still places in America that leave their mark, the father thinks. The kind of mark that can be seen and heard, a type of brand that is pure. The father is deeply branded too, but his scars are inside. They fester. They are unspeakable and dramatic and profoundly interesting. If only he could find the words to express them, they would pour from him like blood from a wound. He does not want to go to the funeral of his old friend and he regrets bringing his son. They were meant to bond, but he sees now they have nothing in common.

The point of view shifts. The son wishes his father weren't so silent. He wishes his father would confide in him. The son has never heard of this friend who has died, but now they are driving fourteen hours to attend the funeral. When he asks his father for a story about the dead man, the father shakes his head. Why does his father speak so easily to the waitress? The father and Midwestern Girl talk about the weather; *funeral weather*, they both agree. Then, before he knows it's happening, the conversation turns to the son.

What this one will never understand, the father says, *is that you don't get to do anything you want.*

You sure don't, Midwestern Girl says. She could not agree more.

The son tries to yell, but he finds himself mute. He tries to stand, but finds he is trapped.

Ha, thinks Midwestern Girl.

I joined the navy when I was seventeen, the father says. *I married a woman I loved and that wasn't enough to make me happy. I didn't like being a father because I was always too tired. I have a collection of magazines specifically for men who like plump women in exotic costumes and my son found it one day and has never been able to forget it and every Halloween he sees witches and Hello Kitties and ladybugs and nurses and imagines me bent over the magazine, and he can't scrub that first image from his mind, that woman with the enormous breasts in a Sherlock Holmes cap, pipe hanging suggestively from her lips, trench coat gaping open to reveal a bustier underneath.*

Rewind the scene.

That road trip with your father was a disaster. You fear you will turn out to be just like him. But no. *The son* fears he will turn out to be like his father. *The protagonist* fears he will never escape this diner, not even if he moves a thousand miles away. Not even if he starts a new life somewhere sunny, where California Girl will teach him to live for the moment. Her breasts will be small and firm and high. You flick your wrist. You crack your knuckles. But the scene refuses to change. California Girl will not be summoned. The diner has linoleum floors. The far-right wall is painted floor to ceiling with a mural of smiling pancakes, hurtling into the air before returning to the red-hot skillet. Never has breakfast struck you with such horror. The woman behind the diner bar is younger than you realized, freckles on her arms, a clip holding up fair but limp hair, and she wears a name tag. Carolyn.

You know, says Carolyn, when his father has gone to the bathroom, *you have me all wrong*. You think she should smile—isn't this the moment when the woman smiles?—but she does not. *I'm not from here at all. I'm from Minneapolis. This is my summer job. I'm an intern at Saddle Creek Records here in Omaha.*

You know Minneapolis is in Minnesota, Omaha is in Nebraska, but that doesn't mean anything. The Dakotas. The Plains. The Prairie. The Badlands. The Driftless Area. You feel the Midwest spread out, form an unfamiliar, unwieldy constellation.

Carolyn drops off your check before you can think of

a question to ask her, about music or short order cooking. She turns away from you, and goes to wait on another customer. Of course, you think, looking around, we are not the only people here.

For a while, you write stories about New York again, but your heart isn't in it.

The protagonist goes to a party and meets no one. He takes a cab uptown and has an unremarkable experience. The East River is still there, but he feels no wild need to scream into its uncaring face. He walks down the street with no particular destination in mind and realizes he's arrived at that sex shop where he once escaped the rain. He goes back inside and the woman is there, still dry. She still says hello and smiles, sifts through that bin of purple butt plugs. But she is not shy. She does not apologize. There is no bachelorette party. She is there to buy a purple butt plug for herself. She doesn't have a niece. Her only sibling, Jason, died in a car accident when she was ten. The woman's name is Kara and her mother calls her Kitty.

Carolyn and Kara are gone, made in a flash of light and shed as quickly as a shadow goes in darkness. If every woman she has ever been were given a name, would there be a Midwestern Girl at all?

———

A man goes to a company picnic in suburban Philadelphia. Midwestern Girl holds hands with the protagonist's rival, a tall blond executive. They look into each other's eyes but don't speak until the protagonist begins to eavesdrop. He has tried all afternoon to resist, to talk with his friend in accounting, to gossip with the women in production, but in the end, the couple pulls him into their orbit. Even at this crucial moment, the rival is given no lines of dialogue. Midwestern Girl caresses his forearm, a caress with which the protagonist will torture himself. She is pretty and, at the moment between thought and smile, beautiful. She is silent *and* mysterious. She opens her lips and says, *I want you to take me home and make love to me.*

She opens her lips and says, *You are twice the man he is.*

It's getting ridiculous.

She opens her lips and says, *I have a bachelors in physics and I am only using this company as a stepping stone to a much better, more important job. I will leave every one of you behind.*

The protagonist flirts with one of the women from production. The woman from production wishes she could capture the attention of Jason from customer service.

The protagonist glances over at Midwestern Girl, this one last time, and to his surprise he finds her looking directly at him, even as she embraces her lover, like she knows exactly what she is doing to him. She flicks her wrist. She cracks her knuckle. She sets the scene.

The protagonist goes to New York City (this, she knows—it is what a protagonist must do), but this time, the protagonist is Midwestern Girl. She wears thick eyeliner, a short skirt, a T-shirt that says "Eagles may soar, but weasels never get sucked into jet engines."

She passes you on the street and strikes up a conversation. Hasn't she seen you somewhere before? Though neither of you can pinpoint how you know each other, it feels as if you've been friends for years. You tell her you have a girlfriend, as if this will disappoint her, but she only smiles. Midwestern Girl invites you and your sort-of girlfriend out for drinks and soon you are all at a basement bar in Brooklyn, laughing and drinking and flirting. When the bar becomes too loud, you suggest you all go back to your apartment, and Midwestern Girl agrees. You and your sort-of girlfriend hold hands on the walk. Midwestern Girl feels her arms swing free at her sides. The evening is fresh and sharp, the summer smell of garbage gone with the first frost. Midwestern Girl accepts the glass of wine you offer—*your home is* lovely, *what a creative use of the space*—and then you and she and your sort-of girlfriend have a three-way.

Isn't that what you hoped for? Afterward, when you cannot sleep, you stare out your window and sip a bourbon—if you are living in that kind of story, or a cheap beer, if you are out of bourbon. You'll think, Midwestern Girl ruined it, with her scruples, her wholesome thighs, those ample breasts that weren't ample at all, a trick of padding, optimism, and the late-afternoon light. You'll think, I don't want to go back to the woman in my bed. Because Midwestern Girl is already gone. She got off twice and left without saying thank you. It is you, not her, who ruminates. It is you, not her, who wonders whether you lost something unnamable when you reached for two women who both turned out to be strangers.

While you gaze out the window, Midwestern Girl is at the Greyhound bus station, buying a ticket home. She eats a slice of bad pizza and pulls her knees to her chest as she sits on the broken plastic bucket seat. It is lucky that she is not waiting for a moment of epiphany, but is simply looking forward to the rock of the bus as it rolls down the highway, and the feeling of the glass as she rests uncomfortable against its cold pressure.

SCENE IN A PUBLIC PARK AT DAWN, 1892

No small sensation has been made by the
report of a duel between two ladies. . . . The
[disagreement] was regarded as so serious
that it could only be settled by blood.

—PALL MALL GAZETTE, AUGUST 23, 1892

We call it an emancipated duel—the duelists, seconds, and doctor, all women—but we will never be emancipated from the stupidity of men.

I am the doctor. In the carriage, I have pads of fabric prepared to stanch the bleeding, and before they fight,

I insist they remove their upper garments. If a rapier pierces muscle, I won't have dirty linen entering with it. The duelists unhook their shirtwaists, untie their under-bodices, fold their chemises over their skirts, leave their steam-molded corsets to lounge on the grass, eerie as the skeletons of whales. All that is left on their lovely ribs are red divots from the places they've been bound.

They breathe deep for the pleasure of it. They shake hands. They strut. They speak. It's all bravado, a script we have read in novels and watched on stage. Is this how men speak? *How dare you. You presume too much. I'll repay your insolence with blood.* They are dueling over a flower arrangement, who copied whom, and it would be easy to think them ridiculous. But I don't. As if flowers are ever only flowers, words only words. As if men duel over anything better, shooting each other over the imaginary flowers we press between our legs. The women move three paces apart. One of them looks a bit pale now that it's beginning in truth; she looks to the side, eyes searching, as if she has expected someone to stop them. They hold their swords high. Who should be the one to say en garde?

———

A blade through flesh is nothing like a needle pricking a finger. When I first cut open a cadaver, I expected the incision alone to crack the chest wide, to open the dead like a cabinet. But it takes strength to crack a sternum and will to get inside.

The duel is quick. The pale woman cuts the other's nose with a wild, panicked swipe. She's shocked at what she's done. The other woman grins, blood on her teeth, and dances forward, cuts a deft slash across the pale woman's arm. First blood to one, but the better hit to the other. Both look happy when I yell that it's done. The women touch their wounds and lick their salty fingers and one of the seconds faints, but not at the blood—though that is what the paper will say—no, she faints at the pleasure on the duelists' faces, the flush across their upper breasts, the strength of their arms, the desire she feels to strip her own clothes off and join them.

Not to be outdone, the other second fakes a swoon. But she's felt lust before, seen blood on her menstrual rags and gushing from her sister as she died in childbirth. They had to burn the mattress, the stain was set so deep. I check her pulse as she lies in the grass and when she glances into my eyes, she looks ashamed of herself.

Honor has been satisfied, I say, and the other women nod. As I bandage an arm, tie a corset tightly back into place, I think that if I were to design a duel, I would not imitate men. What does skill with a sword or a pistol prove about truth or right? Why must half of us always lose? Place the duelers in neighboring rooms and leave them there. Let them grow bored. Give them nothing to do but embroider and nothing to drink but tea. See how long they can stand the silence. See how long it takes before they are whispering through the wall, grateful for the sound of another voice, willing to admit that they were both wrong, willing to admit anything if it will set them free.

HOW TO RETILE YOUR BATHROOM IN 6 EASY STEPS!

1. Plan ahead. Remember, your bathroom will be out of commission for a few days.

Grip the handle of a screwdriver, and wedge its blade beneath the tiles, stab and jam, push down until you hear that pop, until the tile breaks in half and makes an edge sharp enough to cut. You will not cut yourself, obviously. Nothing dramatic is happening. Your fingers are powerful in their yellow rubber work gloves, your hands are steady, your mind is clear. You are ready. The ugly fucking tile is only the beginning of what you'll accomplish. You are coming for the treacherous tub, the affected half-shell sink, the deceitful picture of a sail-boat hanging over the toilet. You hate that picture. You hate all nautical bathroom decor and its insistence that the toilet trigger thoughts of the ocean. You are sure it is the reason your children tried to flush their fish to freedom.

Take a deep breath. Stand and wipe sweat from your forehead with your wrist. Lift the picture off the wall and throw it into the hallway with the rest of the trash. Say, "Fixed." The ghost of the picture remains as a stubborn square of darker green. Do not worry. You will repaint. This has been a long time coming, which is almost the same as being prepared.

2. *Buy supplies.*

Plastic sheeting. Masking tape. Utility knife. Chisel. Hammer. There must be a hammer somewhere, but do not go into the garage to look. You want your own hammer. Chalk-line tool. Thin-Set. Spacers. Level. Wet saw. Tile nippers. Tile cutting bit. Water-resistant silicone caulk.

Do not go to the store to buy these items. You did not bear children so that you could go to the store yourself. Your younger son is in his room fooling around with his girlfriend, who stayed the night. Pretend you do not know this. Pretend you are sending your older son because he is downstairs finishing breakfast, clearly

available, and not because your younger son might refuse to go. Your older son will complain that this is
unfair. He is correct. It is also unfair that your husband
has left you for the orthodontist. It is unfair that he did
not leave you years ago, when you still had many different people you wanted to fuck and many frequent-flier
miles. It is unfair that you never learned how to walk in
heels and unfair that you might need to learn now. It is
unfair that you got a C in that art class in college and
stopped drawing and unfair that your coworker over-
heard you calling her a bitch and unfair that polar bears
are stuck on melting ice floes and unfair that mosquitoes carry malaria and it is unfair and unfair, and your
son will see it in your expression and will not want to
know what you are thinking. He will go quietly to the
hardware store. You believe in not telling your children
about your problems. Well done, you, for keeping that
all inside. You are a good mother. When you have made
this bathroom beautiful, you will be an even better one.

While your son buys supplies, there will be a lull in
the action. Do not let it shake your passion for home
improvement. There is some beer in the refrigerator.
Carry a bottle out to the backyard and take a single sip.
It is morning. It is spring. It is Saturday. The climbing
vines are budding with purple flowers and will pull
down the wooden fence soon if you don't take care of it.

It is too early for beer but it is also too early for drama and this is why you are not crying, you are not prostrate, some absurd caricature of an abandoned woman, no, you are standing in the sun, waiting for step 3 to take charge of your life.

3. Use a chalk-line tool to mark lines for the tile installation. The tub, toilet, and sink will create some challenges, especially for the amateur tile cutter, but do not be discouraged!

The tiles your son brings home are larger than you pictured and less *blue*.

"This is what blue looks like," your son says. He needs a haircut, and you sweep his bangs from his eyes, the better to see him scowl.

The blue looks even worse when you take it into the bathroom. Blame the green paint. Your son informs you that the hardware store did not have a chalk-line tool. He has brought you a yardstick and a box of chalk from the playroom turned guest room turned storage room. This will work fine. Your Norwegian foremothers did not have fancy chalk liners. They laid tile using their eyes and their keen spatial reasoning. They sailed boats using the stars. Their forearms never tired when kneading dough or giving hand jobs. When their husbands fucked orthodontists, they killed them.

Do not remember the many times the orthodontist had her hands in your sons' mouths, stretched their lips as wide as hungry baby birds' beaks. Do not imagine those hands on your husband's body. Do not imagine the two of them in bed, making plans for a weekend of cycling, an activity you've always hated, nothing but a slower, harder way to go somewhere. Worse still, do not imagine them talking about you, discussing how you took the news, indulging in guilt, feeling good about feeling sorry for you. Worst of all, worst beyond anything, is that your husband is a mostly good man, as you are a mostly good woman. You want to call him and tell him you are glad he is gone, that you had been thinking about leaving *him* once the boys were out of the house. You want to call him to tell him to go fuck himself, you want to yell and scream and terrify him, not enough to make him come back, though perhaps that too, but just enough that he begins to wonder what you are capable of, if after all these years you have hidden depths.

Do not do this. He will not believe you have hidden depths. You struggle to believe it yourself.

Instead, put your yardstick next to a piece of tile and

measure it. Measure it again. Write down the measure-
ment to make sure you aren't going to make a mistake.
Now take what you have written, ball it up, and flush it
down the toilet. You are confident. You are not afraid
to make mistakes. You thrive on the unknown. Pick up
your piece of chalk and draw a long white line across
the floor of the bathroom. Draw another and another.
You are the queen on this chessboard. When you are
done—and here is a tricky part—look at the strange
shapes you have made, the places where your perfect
squares run into obstacles and become puzzle pieces.

Feel the weight of the tile cutter in your hand, the
blade like a large X-Acto knife. Draw the cut you will
make on the back of the tile. Measure as best you can.
This can be delicate work. Be firm when you press
down on the blade, but don't be sudden. Do not shatter
a whole tile to remove only a corner.

4. Spread Thin-Set mortar on the
floor. The Thin-Set should be as thick
as the tile you are placing down.

You feel confused, but don't be alarmed. Yes, the Thin-
Set seems like it will hide the chalk lines you spent two
hours drawing. Perhaps this set of directions is not the
best set of directions on the internet. Perhaps you could

have done more research. What is important is that you keep the picture of the lines in your mind. This should be easy to do. Just look at them. Think of all of the things you already have in your mind, things harder to remember. The first five digits of pi. The Gettysburg Address. The address of your first apartment. The way to address a duke or a viscount or a queen, your grace, my lord, your majesty. The smell of pot in your youngest's backpack and the taste of the joint you took from it. The first time you touched your clitoris and the bafflement you felt, how you pressed and poked and wondered if you were broken. The first time you orgasmed, how it wasn't that great, intense but short, the sensation superficial but the victory over yourself sweet. The image of the earth rising over the moon. Your newborn sons, disgusting and beautiful. The tang of milk one day past good. Your father dying suddenly two thousand miles away. Your dog dying in your arms because the vet said it would keep the animal from panicking. The way your husband stood, defiant and guilty, telling you he wanted to be happy. The way he said *in love*. The way he clutched those words to him like a kitten he was proud of saving, like you were the tree he'd pulled it from. The way he held your hip when you couldn't sleep, stroked your hair like your mother used to. The way your mother braided your hair too tight. *Don't squirm like that, Miranda.* The way you laced your sons' shoes too tight, *Don't squirm like that,* double knots, always worried they would trip. After all that, these chalk lines and bathroom tiles are nothing. They will hold you now. They will keep you from panicking.

5. Place your tiles. Be patient,
be gentle. Let them dry in place.

You should not have spread Thin-Set over the entire floor. Look again at the directions. And if the directions were not specific, then you should have been thinking for yourself, thinking a few steps ahead. You are fucking this up. You fuck everything up. This is embarrassing for you. Your children are in their rooms feeling embarrassed for you. Your friends are in their homes feeling embarrassed for you. It is getting dark outside. Your husband is not coming home from his brother's tonight or any other night. Your husband is definitely not at his brother's. You are sleeping alone.

Take off your shoes and socks, and hold a stack of tiles in your arms. Tiptoe across the wet Thin-Set as quickly as you can and climb into your tub. Set the tiles down beside you, then lean out of the tub and place the tiles where you can reach. See? This is not so hard. This is okay. Feel glad that your bathroom is small and your arms are long. Consider giving up and staying in this tub forever. Now leave the tub. Do it now. And don't step on the tiles you have already put down and ruin your work. You will have to stand on the Thin-Set, on the very frontmost balls of your feet, to lay down the tiles around the toilet, the tiles you cut with such care. They fit. It is an enormous accomplishment. They fit almost the way you imagined. Press the tiles down as quickly as you can, and when they are in place, get back out of that bathroom. The patch of Thin-Set near the door looks like small animals have run through it. Your toes are glued together and your feet stick to the carpet. Pull a sliver of tile out of your heel and see how it bleeds only a little and not for long. Kneel, careful of the pile of debris, and lay down those last pieces of tile. Look at that.

Now wait. This is the hardest part. Wait, without losing focus, without asking if this was such a good idea, without feeling too much—you are already so good at this kind of waiting, how different are waiting and continuing to be alive, and if your husband is done waiting, then you are happy for him and so, so angry.

Keep yourself busy while you wait. Go downstairs and check on your children, see that your oldest son has made macaroni and cheese, is feeding his brother, is stepping up, what a good son, you hate that he needs to be a good son, hate *him* for a moment for taking everything on himself, as if this is all about him and not you, not a hurt that can be only yours, a wound you can nurse without worrying about anyone else. Sit down at the table. Smile and ask them if they've had good days. Smile and hold that smile on your face as your oldest holds his. Your youngest doesn't look up from his phone but that doesn't mean he isn't watching. They are waiting too. Feel, for a moment, how much you love them both, feel it too strongly, it feels the same as hating them, feel it so much it would only upset them, feel it until it hurts and you want to run your fingers through their hair and kiss their foreheads and hug them violently, and so instead rise from the table and say, *No rest for the wicked!* like you're Glinda the good fucking witch on a mission from God.

The mess in the upstairs hallway is still there. Someone is going to get hurt. You should really clean it up, and yet you like the chaos of it, the way it embodies you, sustains you even as you realize you are exhausted. You sit on the floor and pick up one shard of tile at a time, dropping them clink by clink into your new plastic bucket. If you were someone else, this might be meditative. From downstairs, you can hear the murmur of your sons' voices but you cannot hear what they say. Your youngest laughs as they clear the table. Soon they come upstairs, say good night to you, on the floor with your bucket, and go into their rooms to press their earbuds in as deep as they will go.

Once you are alone, sit on the kitchen counter and soak your feet in the sink, since you cannot use the bathtub. Watch the hot water flush your calves. Wait to see if the Thin-Set will wash away without taking your skin.

6. *Check to make sure your tiles have set. Wait twelve hours, twenty-four if you can, and then apply the grout in the space between each tile. Let dry.*

You are almost done. You are running down the hill now. Feel the wind at your back, the grass between your toes, the blue jay who sometimes sits on your fence chirping with joy, but do not let this feeling of accomplishment rush you. A good grouting is essential to the long-term health of your bathroom floor. Fill every crack. Check around every tile, level the grout with a wooden coffee stirrer, and when you are sure you have been thorough, set the tub of grout on the ugly half-shell sink.

Look at your work.

It is not any better than the previous bathroom floor.

In fact, it is worse. Your tiles are crooked and do not lie flat. They dip and jut as if riding the last of the wake from a now-distant ship. Your grout work is good. You were careful and diligent. But accept that water will always find a way to sneak between the grout and the tile, between the tile and the floor. That little by little, mildew will grow and rot will eat away at the floor and the floor will get soggier and weaker and a water spot will appear on the ceiling of the living room and you will pretend it is not there and the spot will spread until one day when you are sitting on your couch alone watching television the ceiling will cave in and you will be killed in a shower of not-quite-blue bathroom tiles.

This is a worst-case scenario. This is still years away. Lie down on the cool tile floor. *Your* cool tile floor. Relax. Let your fists clench, then unclench. Relax your toes, your calves, your thighs, your stomach, your neck, and your mouth. Feel that your fingers are weights. Feel every task they have ever performed. Feel them drag your entire body down. And when you think you might finally relax, might accept that the tiles are crooked but still your own, open your eyes to see your oldest son in the doorway. He is worried about you. His hands are shoved into his pockets. He wants and does not want you to speak to him like the grown man he almost is. And maybe that would be best. Maybe you say too little, maybe he is imagining a worse catastrophe, a terminal illness, an asteroid approaching the earth. Maybe, like every child before him, he already knows what's wrong and is simply waiting for you to say it. There are words for this moment—an exact right kind and number—but if you begin to speak, you will never stop. Instead, trace your fingers over the edge of a tile, feeling its corner, sharp enough to cut, and do the best you can.

Say to your son, "Look. I did it."

Say, "I did it all by myself."

Let him think that you think that you did an amazing job.

WE HANDLE IT

We first see him at the reservoir, a middle-aged man with an oval of fur on his chest, nipples like button eyes, and blue swim trunks with yellow Hawaiian flowers. We are swimming, and he regards us from the shore in that way we are learning to expect from a certain kind of man.

Like every day in Tennessee, it is hot. In the early afternoon we walk from the stone campus of this small college to the lake. We are at a summer music camp, our fingertips sore from strings, our backs sticky with sweat, and when we reach the lake we shed our summer dresses and leap from a boulder into the water, which is deep and clean. Around the lake are tall pines and the heavy hum of Southern bug life. We float on our backs, conscious of how our breasts protrude from the water, pleased that we are sixteen, except for Caisa who is seventeen and over-proud of it. For her birthday, she buzzed her head. Her cheekbones are sharp and high, and even if she were not older, she would be our leader because she walks with confidence and draws checkers on the white rubber of her Converse in ballpoint pen. We wish we could go home and buzz our heads, draw on our shoes, but we like our sneakers white, our mothers happy.

The man doesn't jump into the water. He walks down the wooden stairs to the dock, sits, then eases himself into the water as if it pains him. Though we don't say anything, we cease floating on our backs, tucking ourselves under the surface, our heads and shoulders bobbing in a circle.

"It's like, what is he doing here?" Becca says, and we nod. We watch from the corners of our eyes as he swims the edge of the lake. Though we are the outsiders, we resent him. Today this is our lake, and we are loud and selfish. When we walk down sidewalks, we take up the entire path.

"Shouldn't he be at work?" Megan says.

"Maybe we should go," Lisa says, but no one agrees. Lisa is timid. Lisa braids her blond hair so tight her skull stretches her skin.

When Caisa gets bored of watching the man, she

declares that we are going to take over the floating dock. She wants to sunbathe. We swim over and one by one go up the metal ladder, the rungs slick on our feet, water sluicing down our limbs. It is so warm that we don't even shiver. We deliberately don't check to see if the man is looking at us, though he must be, because we are young and nearly naked in our triangle-top bikinis and our bodies are powerful in at least this one way, that they contain—exude—something which is desired.

We lie side by side. We know we'll burn.

"It's hot," says Lisa.

"Who do you think the trumpet player would fuck? If he had to," says Megan.

"Not you," says Caisa.

"I walked in on my parents having sex once," says Becca.

We giggle, uncomfortable and a little proud. We have all done this. It is the only time our mere presence has struck our parents dumb.

With our eyes closed, we smell the algae on the wood, we smell the sunlight and it makes our noses itch. We feel the dock dip and just like that the man's shadow comes over us. He stands on the top rung of the ladder. He is old, at least in his forties, with a body that reminds us of our fathers, a belly perched on skinny calves.

"You ladies from that music camp?" he asks.

We think about sitting up, but we are conscious of our stomachs, skin that will pooch and crease. We feel the wisdom of deer, who know how to remain perfectly still.

"I've seen a bunch of you. You're everywhere in those name tags."

Caisa rises to her elbows.

"Your parents make you come to this camp? What instruments do you play?"

"Violin," says Megan.

"Viola," says Lisa.

"Cello," says Becca.

"Harp," says Caisa, but that's not true and we feel stupid because we've forgotten that we can be anyone here, play make-believe, slip in and out of fantasies; we don't owe anyone the truth. Though we want more, we tinker only with our smallest dreams, tiny corrections to our hair and personalities. Megan pretends to be cynical. Becca pretends everything is funny. Lisa pretends she'd rather be with us than be alone. Caisa need not pretend, we think, but she lies most easily of all.

"Where y'all from?" the man asks, and we are quick learners.

"Florida," says Megan from Maine.

"New York," says Lisa from Oregon.

"Paris," says Becca from Los Angeles, and we feel she's overdone it.

"Nashville," says Caisa from Florida.

"Local girl," says the man, and Caisa smiles.

Through his wet swim trunks, we think we can see the shape of his dick, though it may be how the fabric is bunching. We shouldn't be looking at what we don't want to see, but we can't help ourselves, and once we look, we feel certain he's noticed. We fear we have agreed to something and we want to look again.

"You're beautiful young things," he says.

"We have class soon," Caisa says.

"School's important," the man says and smiles like he's said something else. "You girls have a good one." With that, he lowers himself back into the water.

We are silent as he swims away.

"What a creep," Becca says.

"Totally gross," Megan says.

Caisa pulls her arms over her head and stretches, as if she still owns her skin. When we stand, we leave wet prints of our bodies on the wood.

We tell the others at camp about the creepy man. We are not the least popular, but we are not the most popular, and our story gives us stature. We are like birds who, hearing a footfall, call out, pass their fear from tree to tree. At every telling, the man becomes more pathetic, and we laugh until we feel almost sorry for him. What other animal passes on the call of danger and feels a thrill of pleasure?

Two days later, it is almost curfew. We hurry home from the library, cutting across quadrangles as the clouds blow fast across the sky and the wind warms our legs like a panting dog. Under our feet, the ground is saturated from a day of rain. Pine needles and fallen leaves smell dark, fecund, when we kick them up. Mosquitoes bite us. Our arms collect scratches from when the itch becomes too much. Lisa already has thin scars on her inner thighs, raised and orderly. We do not mention them.

We don't see the man until we are too close to turn around. He's sitting on the low stone wall outside the dorm, his hairy legs kicked out, blocking the sidewalk.

Megan taps Caisa, who taps Becca, who taps Lisa, who pinches her face.

Here is the secret that everyone knows: we are easy to frighten. We have seen the videos about stranger danger, friend danger, and boyfriend danger. Husband danger and father danger. But we are proud. More important, we don't want to be the one who fails us all by running away.

The man tips his baseball hat. "Storms moving through," he says. His beard is a shadow on his face.

We look to the sky, to check if there is some explanation there, something he has come here to show us. But it's the same clouds, the same shifting patchwork of stars. "We'll get more rain before it stops for good," he says.

We wear our silence as a shield.

He chuckles and stands, still in our way. "I've never seen a girl with one of these," he says, and we realize he is talking to Caisa. He runs his hand over her buzzed head, his thumb grazing her ear, and even Caisa seems too surprised to respond. "Suits you," he says, and then he moves aside, just enough that we can pass him in a single file line. The last one into the dorm pulls the door shut and keeps pulling, though we've already heard the lock catch.

In our shared suite after lights out, we play our fear, finding its chords. The air-conditioning blasts and the sweat on our backs is cold.

"I think he's still out there," Megan says. She sits cross-legged. Next to her on the bed, Lisa leans against the wall, rolling a wooden whistle, a carving of a tortoise, over and over in her hands.

"We should tell someone," Lisa says.

"Loitering is a crime," Becca says. "You can't loiter wherever you want."

"I'm sure he's still out there. Can't you feel it?" We can feel it. We are sure he is still out there. "Should I look out the window?" Megan asks.

"He'll see you," Lisa says.

"I don't care," Megan says, but she doesn't move. From the beds, we can see the tree outside the window, lit from below by a yellow streetlight. We are glad our room is on the third floor and that the man is too large to climb the tree's delicate limbs.

"He could be a serial killer," Becca says.

We sit with this in our imaginations. He murders the girls who have come before us, one group each summer, at first flautists, because they are the prettiest, until he realizes that oboists are trusting and bassists have the biggest instrument cases, perfect to fill with rocks. He ties the heavy black cases to their limp ankles; the girls won't float when he throws their bodies into the deep lake. We imagine he has a basement full of instruments now, his own hidden orchestra.

"Back in my hometown," Megan says, "there was this guy who lived in a cabin. He lived there with his wife, but one fall she died in a car accident, t-boned by this cheerleader, chick drunk as all fuck when she did it. So he was all alone through the winter. And the winter is long in Maine. Like real long. Everyone in town wonders if he's dead or lost his mind, and after the first thaw the sheriff goes to check. When the sheriff drives back, he doesn't say a word, packs up his bags, and leaves town. Then the diner owner, a man with thick arms, goes to the cabin. He comes back and tells his wife and daughters they are moving to New Mexico, where he's heard life is easier. No one else goes out there, not for months, until one night, two cheerleaders do it on a dare, or because they're stupid, I'm not sure. They get to the cabin. There's a faint light on inside. They creep up the steps in their tiny cheerleader skirts and tiny cheerleader tops, and when they open the door, they see the man sitting at his table, normal as you like, doing a cross-word puzzle. Hey, they say, and when he turns to them, they see that he's missing the skin over half his face, the flesh over half his ribs, his left arm rotting away. He'd been eating himself, bit by bit, all winter. And when he sees their uniforms, he grabs them and ties them up and devours them *piece by piece* all through the next *winter!*" Megan yells the last part as she grabs Lisa, who shrieks.

"That isn't funny," Lisa says.

"That is the worst ghost story I ever heard," Becca says.

"That guy's wife really was killed by a cheerleader,"

Megan says. "But at the end of the winter he was just skinny."

We feel sad imagining this man, but mostly we feel the romance of his suffering, how much he must have loved his wife, how much we want a man to suffer for love of us. "The first football game that next fall," Megan says, "he put arsenic in the Gatorade cooler. Football players and cheerleaders all dropped dead, pom-poms, orange paper cups, and bodies scattered on the sideline."

"You are so full of shit," Becca says, but she doesn't sound sure.

"Think what you want," Megan says.

Caisa lies with her legs up the wall. "You think he's smart, or is he stupid?" she says, as if we haven't been speaking at all. "Our guy. That makes all the difference."

Stupid seems better, because we are smart. But if we're so smart, perhaps we can think most like the smart man. The stupid man—what to expect? The stupid man, as we imagine him, is slow and plodding but carries a cleaver and breaks down the door in the night, his act so senseless that we have no defense. We shiver, and as if we've called him, a pebble raps against the window, the sound short and sharp, and as we begin to think it's nothing, something strikes the glass again.

Lisa begins to cry. Not loud. We know bad things have happened to Lisa.

"Do you think that's him?" Becca whispers, as if he can hear us.

"Who else would it be?" Megan says.

"We have to tell someone," Becca says. "I'm not joking, you guys. We have to tell a counselor."

"What do you think a counselor will do?" Caisa asks. Her question is genuine. She sits up, calm, curious.

"Call the police," Becca says. We nod.

"I bet, if we call, he gets away with it," Caisa says. "I bet he does this all the time. I bet he says he wasn't doing anything wrong. I bet he says we're hysterical. I bet he says we're looking for attention."

We bet he has a girlfriend somewhere. We bet he treats her badly, but she doesn't leave him. We bet he is friends with some of the local cops. We bet he drinks beer with them. We bet he beats his wife. We bet his son hates him. We bet his son will be like him. We bet he has been arrested but never charged. We bet he is lonely. We bet he is both smart and stupid. We bet he knows how to spike a girl's drink. We bet we know how this story will end.

We will walk out of our dorm room and sneak down the dark hall.

We will go to the kitchen, where a week ago we made

potato salad for the Fourth of July. In a drawer are the large knives; when we used them, they stuck in the wet starch, the potato half cleaved. We will each take a knife. The handles will be black with silver studs, cool in our palms, like our mothers' knives. When we think about our mothers, we will be angry with them.

We will look outside at the sidewalk, but the man won't be there.

We will leave the dorm, circle it, but we won't find him.

We will walk away from the dorm, down the middle of the road that leads into town. We won't hurry. We know he will follow. Our bodies will bring him to us, our breasts and our hips, the scents under our arms and between our legs. When we hear him, his footsteps behind us on the asphalt, we'll pretend we don't. Instead, we will look to the sky and see that the rain he promised has not come. We will smile to see the clouds gone and our smiles will bare our teeth and we will feel our anger well up from our bones, a pressure beneath our skin that feels like power, anxious and hot, and we will hold this heat inside of us until he is close enough that we smell him too, gunpowder and exhaust. The first sound he hears will be Becca's laughter, as she realizes that what we feel is joy, and when we turn to face him, our hair will burst into flames and we will light up the empty road, our fire glinting off our knives, and we will see that we have struck him dumb, that he feels fear but, more importantly, awe, and when we stab him he will give, not like a potato, but an orange: a little resistance from the peel, but the flesh inside easy to divvy up, a bitter piece for each of us.

Acknowledgments

First and again and again, thank you to my agent Sarah Burnes for reading my stories and believing there was a collection here, long before that collection was actually finished. In your life, you walk the walk of your convictions, and inspire me to the do the same. Second, and with the same infinite gratitude, to my editor Margaux Weisman, for taking on this book and making it better with your sharp eye and your incredible enthusiasm. Thank you to Lydia Ortiz for the phenomenal cover. I aspire to writing stories worthy of its flames.

To the journals and editors who have published my stories, thank you for championing the work of emerging writers and including me in their ranks. A special thank-you to *SmokeLong Quarterly* and Tara Laskowski and Christopher Allen, who published "Shit Cassandra Saw . . ." and, with their love and support, opened my eyes to all of her possibilities.

This book is for my teachers: Linda Welzig, Greg Smith, Susan Jaret McKinstry, George Shuffleton, Andrew Fisher, Alice McDermott, Jean McGarry, Chris Bachelder, and Michael Griffin. A special thanks to Leah Stewart, my teacher and mentor, who understands novel structure better than anyone I've ever met and sets an example for how to live as a strong, funny, unapologetic woman, writer, and all-around badass.

For my Sewanee family, who are too many to name, and especially the Sewanee staff, especially especially the #SWCBar, Ananda Lima, Chris Poole, and Dan Groves; and Adam Latham, my office ride-or-die; and Shelby Knauss, who let me buzz off all her hair that night. The Sewanee Writers' Conference and Sewanee Young Writers' Conference changed the trajectory of my life.

For my very oldest friends, who taught me that friends were also family: Belinda, Carolyn, Jordie, Lisa, Scott, and Tom. I could have been a weird kid without you all, but I would have been a lonely one. I love you.

For my Hopkins and Cincinnati cohorts, who read many of these stories but mostly read far worse ones and helped me grow: Jocelyn Slovak, Alex Creighton, Emily Parker, Courtney Sender, Brenda Peynado, and Ryan Ruff Smith.

For Joselyn Takacs, a beautiful writer and beautiful spirit, intrepid explorer, and incredible cook, I can't wait for our next adventure. You bring the moleskin, I'll bring the superglue.

For Molly Read and Juli Case, two of the strongest people I have ever met. You aren't just incredible writers; you are incredible women and loyal friends. The next time we're at the fish tank bar, the first round is on me.

For Dan Paul, a dear friend from that first puddle jump. I wish every Wednesday was running, funny pool, and wine club. You made your home, with Brett and Ava, my home, and made my time at Cincy creative, rich, and frequently hilarious. #BearcatDestiny This book wouldn't exist without you. Or it might, but it would be way worse.

For Arlo and Alice, who at some point will briefly think their aunt is cool. I'm excited for that window and plan to buy lots of scarves. I can't wait to know you both as you grow into yourselves.

For my parents, who read to my sister and me every night and filled our home with books. I have you to thank for making me a reader and for letting me know that the world was within reach, if I had the courage to go and grab it.

For my husband, Andrew, whose love is behind everything I do, filling me up, keeping me going. Having you at my side makes everything possible.

And finally, for my sister Claire. If I were a better writer, I'd say something to perfectly encapsulate everything you mean to me, but why bother, when you already know.